Devious Indulgence

All about the evil there is

R. L. (RICK) HUTCHINS

ISBN: 978-1-957009-26-1 (hc)
ISBN: 978-1-957009-27-8 (sc)
ISBN: 978-1-957009-28-5 (e)

Library of Congress Control Number: 2022902619

Contents

Acknowledgement

****

Giving honor, to the most high God, in which my help, does come from, that made heaven and earth. To my dearest mother in, who has motivated me, to doing my best, at what I have being doing. And for a bright and healthy future, I must stay, the course, that I am on. All my successfulness, comes, from the very same God, that made everything, that we can far imagine. I like, to thank, all my family and friends, for their support. And those, that inspired me as well. In always, remember, to do everything, by faith and not by sight. Therefore, only God, knows, the heart, the mind and souls of men.

We as a Generation, that can overcome, various situation, as evil can outweigh, the good in us. Then good, will after all prevailed. Follow your dreams, and don't let excuses, hinder your plans, as moving forward. We struggle, we are frustrated, with time and life itself, as it progressive. That when we all, needs a helping hand. May God, continue, to smile upon us, as his children and enjoy reading, this book, and may God's blessing continually flow.

Hidden Act

Chapter I

Now that Terra, has escape, that group home, that she, was confined too, wasn't keeping her. With the help, she trusts, has escaped with her as well. So going, underground, she can stay low key, for more plotting, to her plans, for fulfillment. Now there's an APB, for young fugitives, which are dangerous and capable of killing, by surprise. Terra is, on an appetite, for destruction and a taste, for revenge, for her father death.

Terra knows, that in, her eyes, her father isn't, wrong for wanting, to kill, the Bentford's. So, where he failed, Terra thinks, she ought, to finished, what he, has started, without any mistakes. Her plot has, to be very precise, with accuracy dead on. Terra needs, for Sam, to be in, the right, place at the right time, for her help, to carried out Sam's demised. So Terra and company will stage, a hit on, Jon while he's not paying any attention, to his surrounding, like he always does.

Now it's a years later, that Ed's being gone, from the evil, that he has establish in his offspring. And Terra is, ready, to kill by all means necessary. And the three, individual, will be no easy job, to handle. But this strong and tight knitted family isn't lying still, for a few renegades, who wants, to destroyed, their loving family, like her father tried. Ed may have, gotten June but the love, this family has is, very strong love, for each other, to be there, for one another's aches and pains. And not let evil, inside at all. So Terra, needs, for a plastic surgeon, to come in, for a new facial makeover, to seal her identity. Put on a wig, to hide everything, from the public. She doesn't want no one, to figure out, who she really is, but someone of importance, like a representative, from the county hospital.

Now the young fugitives, has found, an underground tunnel, to abandon warehouse, for meetings, to goes over, their first endeavor. And Terra know, shortly, that Sam's health is bad, from, the last time, she checked. So, she needs, to report, to the hospital, after her henchman, pays Sam a visit, and create an accident, to get him there. Terra, sends her henchman, to Sha'vore county, to see if Sam is, there. "But don't do anything as of yet." said, Terra. Terra knows, that Jon maybe there, as well. So Terra, has her henchman, to pose as a utility worker, for Lajunta Power& Lights (LP&L). "If, Sam is alone, can you bring, him to me, or do you need help?" ask, Terra. "A short, old man, I think, I can handle him, Ms. Terra." said, the henchman. "Oh, his son is, a little bigger, then you, so be careful." said, Terra.

Now Terra's henchman is, Bobby Raoul, who is a Latin psychopath, that was a security officer, that got fired, for letting Terra, seduce him, while on duty. Ever since, Terra has him, around her finger. To Bobby, she is, the boss, and that's how he sees her. Terra's female protégé is, no other, then Dana Lynn, the one, that has Terra's back, matter what. To Dana, Terra is, the Queen. On Terra's signal, Dana wants, Sheila as bad, as Terra wants her. But last Cain Gordillo is, a handyman, that knows Bobby, from back in, the day, from stealing cars, to working security, with Bobby as well. Terra has given him a nickname (C.G) for short.

Now it's time, to get, to work, with each individual is, really unique, in some kinda way. But they rather, be on, the wild side of, things. So, getting ahead of, things, this is, how someone, would think, by getting a deadly thing accomplished. But no one, has a right, to take, someone else's life. But they do, and it's easy, to do. Now this is, where things get a little sloppy. Because, Terra, has left a few details, out of, the plans, that Bobby, isn't aware of. That the Bentford's, are a family, that will point, a gun, at you, if not recognized, coming, to their porch, and unannounced. Just as a king, would kill you, if someone would show up unannounced in, his courts. Well, that's the Bentford's, for you.

Now Terra, and Bobby, are going over a line of words, to get up on, the Bentford's property, to recognized, each Bentford in, the house. "Bobby, don't mess, this up, I need, these people as I misses, my father." said, Terra. "I'm going, to use Dana, for to get Jon. "And Cain, for Sheila, that b—ch! Blackened my eyes!" said, Terra. "You see I need, these people dead, they took my father, from me! so an eye, for an eye, tooth, for a tooth!!" Aaaaugh!!" as Terra, gets upset, for thinking about her father, being killed in, front of her. "These peasants! Making me sick, for thinking about all this, if only, they let my father kill, Sam's precious daughter. I wouldn't be here, to do this!" said, Terra.

So, the plans, are active, as Bobby set out, to get Sam and deliver him, to the boss Terra. Finding, the words, to lured, him, to kill him first, to get the prize, that is Sheila and Jon. Which are last, to kill off. "Oh Bobby, here's the address, which is, 7765 County Route Rd." said, Terra. Now that Bobby is, headed, to the Bentford's residences, to scope out, the place, to try, to grab, Sam, but it won't be easy, as it looks. So, with a van, with all types of, gidgets and gadgets, to place inside and outside as well, again for Bobby, messing with the Bentford's, could be a last, resort. Because, things have change, since then. Now here comes, the wolves in, sheep's clothing, as evil put on, it's best disguise ever, for more chaotic terror, with a twist of fate. Sam hasn't seen, his brother-in-law, for years, but he talks, to him quite often. His brother-in-law is, from Hawaii, who loves it, over there. Benjamin Tills is his name. He was coming, for June's funeral, but he became sick, and to sick, to travel. Ben is called that, for short, but Ben, loves fishing and bowling. And Sam is, expecting him, next week, for a while. Because, Ben, just retired, a few years back, now and ready, to come, to check up on, the family. Ben's former line of, work was, a detective, for the Honolulu police department in, what he loves about the law enforcement. With Benjamin, coming, to stay awhile is, some relief, that Jon could have, thou with Sam's health isn't the greatest, but Sam tells it, he seen, better days, then worst.

Now that Bobby, has arrived, at the Bentford's place, he looking, to park, a little closer, to the house. But the road is, as narrow, as it gets. So, he parks, across, from the house, which is, a corn field, that someone else owns, up the road. And Bobby, is being sloppy already, by parking in front of, the house, and parking on someone else's property. Bobby isn't thinking well enough, not to get caught. As Jon, peeps out, to see who's parking in, front of the house, across, the street just sitting there, casing, the house. So, Jon, showed, himself out on, the front porch, with his glock at his waist, for comfort, just if any, thing jumps off. So, Jon, is definitely paying attention, this time around, with Sam coming, to the door, to see what has Jon's attention. Sam decides, to step out on, the porch as well. Then Bobby, gets out of, the vanned walks over, to the Bentford's, to let them know, that he is checking on the utility poles in, the area. "Sorry guy's I'm just, a utility guy, checking for damage wires." said, Bobby. "Oh ok!" said, Jon. As Jon and Sam, both goes back into, the house.

Now that, Bobby has saw, what he came, there for, he will return, to get it, for sure. As Bobby, goes back, to his van, to get in, Sheila pulls up into, the driveway, and get out, with grocery, to take into, the house. And Bobby, grabs, his camera to take a picture of, Sheila, from a distance. With her photo, Bobby, kept, looking and gazing at her photo. "Damn, you look good girl." Bobby's thoughts. Bobby knows, that this is, the nemesis of his boss, so he has to be careful, or end up dead. As Sheila, returns, from the store, to put dinner on, Sam comes in and deliver some good news, that uncle Ben is, coming, to stay awhile, with them. "I talk with him, for almost an hour of two." said, Sam. "Oh by, the way, who was, the guy in the van, when I pulled up; across the street?" ask, Sheila. "That's the guy, from, the utility company." said, Sam. "Hey honey, did you bring back, a newspaper?" ask, Sam. "Yes Dad, I got it right here." said, Sheila. With all four individuals', made front page, headlines. "Look at here? There's Ms. Terra, and these three people. "Jon! Come here, for a moment!" said, Sam. "Yeah Dad," said Jon. "Don't that, looks like the guy, that was across, the street, minutes ago?" ask Sam. "He can, pass, for him, absolutely", said, Jon. So going, after the family, would be a mistake, soon enough, with Bobby has already, been identified, from the media. So, another approach must be taken, with one's identity being compromised.

Soon enough, there will be quarrel's among, the group, for simple mistake, that is, called by Terra herself. But making tough decisions, without thinking, could lead, to disaster. Terra, doesn't have experience in, calling shots. For a woman, like her, has a tough time, even comprehending, to her own plans and plots. As Terra, starts, to look at her crew, to see who is faithful, and just as loyal, to her. One in particular, that is Bobby, Terra has, to watch Bobby, around other females, inmates, at the time, when she was locked up. But Terra, knows, that her temper tantrums can get, the best of her, while hiding, from the law.

As Bobby, pulls inside, the lair, he goes straight, to the Queen herself, to give a report, on what happen and what he saw. As for Terra, she needs, detail by detail. Then Terra ask Bobby, for the camera, to see if anything, was on it. Bobby, just had remember, that he only, took a photo of Sheila's body. Bobby hand it, Terra, the camera, then walks, to the restroom, then Terra, lost it, when she saw Sheila's photo. "Bobby!!!" Terra, calls. "What in the f—k!! man!!" said, Terra. "Hey! What is the big deal, Terra!?" ask, Bobby. "You have, this b-t-h photo, on my camera!!" said, Terra. "Ok! Guy's!!calm, the heck down." said, Dana. As Dana, comes, to Terra's defense, "To say that he just being, a man girl", said, Dana. Bobby, look at his boy Cain, for some help, but Cain, paid none attention, to neither Bobby or the ladies. Now feet, has being step on, lines have also been cross. So here comes, repercussions, for the consequences, that Bobby has chosen. Going against, a woman, like Terra, is like committing suicide or maybe signing, your death certificate. Now or later, Terra and along with her protégé, Dana, both women are willing, to make things right, in the latter weeks, to come.

As both women, gazed at Bobby, without a smile or smirk, just like a python, would sizes you up, to get you when not, expecting, to be eaten. That's how Terra, operates, she isn't going, to tell you, that she is going, to get you, she just does it. So why, would you negotiate, with your enemy? When they are trying, to rubout a trouble, which is you. Now Bobby, is going, to watch, his own back, because, he knows, for sure, that both women, works swiftly together like salt and pepper, to savory a taste. Bobby isn't putting anything pass them both. One will kill, at will, the other will slit, your throat, with the one hold you, for the other, to get you, for both women, to finished, you off. Bobby knows, not to trust Cain, for sure now. He might be the one, that tries to rub Bobby out. All Bobby knows, is that none of, them can be trusted. Since he messed up, for taking a photo of, Terra's enemy. But Bobby has, a weapon, if Terra decides, to kill him, before getting out and come clean, with the law. Bobby thought, to go and tell the cops, where they all are at, just to be safe, on his side. And paid, another visit, to the Bentford's residences, to tell the truth, and why he was over there. And minutes later, Cain has approached, Bobby, to let him know, that he needs, to watch his back, because, both of these girls, are going, to get you. Bobby's thought's, were on, the money exacts. Bobby knows, it's not going, to be easy, getting out, this second. But making it, to the door, and run like hell as Bobby thought or go and talk, to Terra.

As Terra, and Dana, approached Bobby, for apology, with both women, with weapons aimed, to shoot, Bobby knows, it's too late, lights out, game over. (Pow! Pow!) (PANG! POW!). Bobby lying dead, shot and killed in cold blood. But Cain, didn't tell Bobby, his number, was up as of, today. Cain, only told, Bobby, to beware of the repercussions. And that was the Terra's way of, solving her trouble's quick and in a hurry. There's no it's, and's and but's about it. Either you in or your dead. Now as Cain, takes Bobby body, to the back, of this underground, which is a steam plant, that runs under parts of, the city. But Cain dumps his old friend, from back in the day, body in this large septic tank, with gross sewage waters from, the city and other parts of Sha'vore county. As standing there looking down into a large hole of water, that smells so gross, thinking when will, the ladies, turned on him. So, Cain, has a thought of taking, Dana first, because, him and Dana, works closely together. So, when Dana, is workout, Cain's thoughts are to come from, the back and then executed. But Cain knows, it would be hard, to do with Terra and Dana, are with one another. And Terra, has come, so trigger happy, to find a mistake, to shoot someone. That her old man's mentality, that she has taken, from his genes, evil is the way, and her life is more happier, when she is plotting dangerous ways to planning evil thoughts. But her planning, and her plotting needs work. With both women, watching Cain, from a distance, with guns at their sides, their thoughts, were to get rid of the guys, and just be the women way. But Dana, told, Terra, that would be a bad ideal, we need a guy's strength, to lift certain things. "So, we will, not kill him just as yet." said, Dana. "Cain!" Terra, calls. "Listen, we need, for you, to go and get food, for us, to eat." said, Terra. "Like from where?!" ask, Cain. "I don't think, none of us, have any money, so how am I getting food Terra?!" Cain, ask. Terra, and company, are suffering another blow, without any nourishments, Terra and her crew, would die, for being on, the run, from the law. "Hey I got a great idea that we can eat." Dana, said. "Cain! I need, for you, to run me to the nineteen market, someone in there, owes, me a favor." Dana, said. "Ok." Cain, said. "Oh yeah, don't get caught." Terra, said.

The Apple
Chapter II

Now that Terra, is all alone, to herself, to think, if her father, was still alive, what would, he says about all of, this. But she, tried, to exercise, her powers, when no one's around. Her eyes change colors again, with her finger nails, came out a few inches, and her hair thicken on her head. But one problem, she doesn't know how, to reverse, her powers, afterword's. But she did, something, that is forbidden, that is, stay away, from water. Terra had put, a little water on, her face, in which causing an irritation and a loss of power. Terra's hair shrinks a couple of inches, her finger nails stay, the same, with one eye was green, and the other light brownish, made her look like she had, Heterochromia iridium. The water signals a clean purification of good and wholesome. Evil can't mix, with good, and not suffer. So, Terra, has to let her powers, wear off, to go back normal. And with Dana and Cain, coming back she needs, to hide her face, from her crew. Within sometimes it's not, good, to reveal, certain things in, life just as of yet.

A day, time and place, when Terra will reveal, her trait's, to her friends. But to them, she a normal human being, with a temper tantrum, at times; when stuff doesn't go her way. Terra acts, just like her father Ed. Ed was well dislike, because he was a smart kid, but he was, to soft. Then his evil ways changed all of, that in one night, as he makes an oath, with the Prince of evil, to do evil, bad and no mercy as he put it. And his powers, were granted, to him, for him. So, you see, that Terra inherited, her powers, from her father's genes. She's had everything accepted, the power, to go invisible, but she will over time. But in, the meantime, she needs, to hide her face, from Dana and Cain. Terra is, not trying, to freak anyone out, with her hair and eyes. This is just a side, that no one has seen as of yet. This is also, why her father, couldn't be around any water, of the sort. Because, he knew, what will happen, if any water would touch him, his powers couldn't reverse, if he wanted it too. Terra thought, that it adds character, to keep, from getting caught. But her evil side, doesn't know, any better, it just knows, it's supposed, to kill, when it's in that state of mind.

But Terra, sat and thinking, wandering why her, and not someone else, that could have been a bearer of evil. Instead, it's her, that her mother's and father's DNA pass to her. But believe it or not, Terra is thinking about all the good, that she could do. Therefore, she can't, because, of her hatred and evil can't allowed that, to happen. With both parents' gone, no other sibling, to talk too, no offspring, to tend too. What a f—king life, I have. Terra thoughts. So that's why, the apple is, so bitter, then sweet. She was the apple of her father's eye, the apple, that failed, but not far, from the tree. Terra was a sweet little girl, when she was an infant, then a toddler, she grew enormously, then your average girl. Then in her teens, she became a woman, the next go around. Terra wasn't your normal female figure. Because, the parasite, that her daddy has spreaded, to her, at birth. The parasite, which made her ability, to overcome several obstacles in school.

Now that Cain and Dana, has returned, from the store, with groceries, they walk in, and sense something is, wrong with, their leader. Terra had her, back turned and her head covered for whatever reason, had Cain and Dana in, suspense in, the way she was looking. Both Cain and Dana, just stood there gazing, at Terra's behavior, and knowing something doesn't look right. "Hey give me, a minute, I'll be right back!" Terra, said. As Cain and Dana, looked at one another, wandering what the hell is, Terra's problem. As Cain told, Dana, that he would help her, with putting, the groceries up. So, while both Cain and Dana conversing, with one another, Terra walks, in, with an attitude, from out of nowhere, with, Cain and Dana.

"What took you both so long, to get f—king grocery?" ask, Terra. "Relax! We tried, not to get caught, with the authorities, looking, for us." said, Cain. "Are you being, or trying, to be smart, with me?" ask Terra. "Tee! What's wrong, with you?" ask, Dana. "You ask, for us, to go and get groceries, now you, jumps our ass, for it, so what kinda s—t is, that?" ask, Dana. "Sorry! I'm under a lot of pressure, being in a state of killing myself." said, Terra. "Girl! I'm not going, to let you, do that, to yourself." said, Dana. Dana Lynn is, a little older, then Terra, by three years. Dana was a manager, for a fast-food chain, until one day, a family of six came into, the restaurant, to eat. But they all were, a father and his five sons, as they sat and jokingly, playing with Dana's, female employee, by touching and fondling her, out of disrespect. Until the female employee, wanted, to quit. But Dana, had other plans for daddy and his five boys'. Dana went, to her car, for a moment, and then returned. She gave, the men, a chance, to make it right, by giving, her female employee an apology. So, the men told, Dana, that they, are the ones, that needs an apology, from her and her female employee. Seconds later all, six men lay dead in their own blood. So, Dana knows, how, to use a fine piece of, metal, like the men in her family. Each one, knows, one's gifts. "Ok! Let's concentrate, on getting, this family, out of my life, for good." said, Terra. "Listen! We are, going, to drive, by the Bentford's place, so I can see, what's new and what we will be going, up against." said, Terra. "So be prepared, to go." said, Terra. "By the way, you are, a beautiful, blessing, to me girl." said, Dana. As getting ready, to pay an unknown visit, over at the Bentford's place, Cain prepared, the van, for the trip. Terra and her protégé, were working on, their appearance, so no one can identify, them in public. "Hey! You both, ready!?" ask, Cain. As both, Terra and Dana, coming, with heavy coats, with wigs and makeup on, asking "How do, we look?" ask Terra. "You both look like, a couple of apples in my sight." said, Cain. While both women giggle, at what was said. Terra needed, a new name, for herself, when out in public. So, she wanted, to be called, "The Apple" because, she is precious in the eyes, of any man, with every man, wants a taste, of her. And envy, from every woman, there is. Terra is putting herself, and her crew, at risk, for going, pass, the Bentford's place. But she is, pointing everyone out, for her crew, to come in, to do the job, that is, needed. That is, to grab Sam, for a ransomed hostage, for a sacrifice, for killing, her father. But if getting, to Sheila, first, that would be even sweeter. Terra, doesn't really want a hostage, she on the other hand is, to kill the people she was once close too. For her father's way, to eliminate his enemy. And she is, still needs, to uphold, her father ways. By killing, that is. Now as getting prepared, to go and scope, the Bentford's home out, they loaded, their weapons, just in case, of some static, may occur, with law enforcement. Or with the Bentford's whichever may come first. Just the thought, of her father, being gone, is a disturbing and despises way, to think, it's makes Terra's hatred, strife, malice, and lasciviousness, can rip her apart, because, she is, hurting inside continually. Terra, never had anyone, to sit her down, to explained, to her about being any good, to others, being good as well, as to yourself.

"Hey Cain, we need, to stop, at my father's place, before going onto the Bentford's." said, Terra. Now this is, really risking all that they, are pushing for. But she goes, and finds, a lot, that can push her wellbeing, to tremendous levels. As they pulling up in, the driveway of, her father's old house, all three get out, to go in, and look around, for stuff, that Terra could use. "Wow, Terra, this is, your father's place?" ask, Dana. "Yup." said, Terra. As Terra, walks into, her father's bedroom, and found more guns, and ammo. But she came across a big jar, of serum, with a note on it, said "Invisible Potion" and she grab, that, like she knew, what that was, but doesn't have a clue. Terra would give, that parasite, that's within her, the ability, to go invisible, at any time. Soon of enough, that parasite will want, to come out, like it did her father. Some days Ed, almost couldn't contain it. This parasite is, itching, to do what it is, supposed to do, that is to, kill what is necessary. So then, Terra, will become very dangerous, even to her crew. "Terra! What's in, the jar?" Cain, ask. "My medicine." Terra, said. "Wow. It looks like milk." Dana, said. "Dana! Shut up!" Terra, said. "I'm sorry, Tee, I didn't mean, to make you mad." said, Dana. While they are inside, this abandon property, there's a Sheriff deputy, that pass the property, looking, for suspicious activity, as he turns around, to check out the property of Ed Dart, there's a van sitting in, the driveway.

Cain glances out, of the window of, the living room, and see this deputy, coming up on, the porch. All three Dana, Cain, and Terra pulled, their weapons, to eliminate, the deputy. The deputy, notice, that the door is opened, and he hears movement inside, as he returned, to his cruiser, for some backup. Before he can reach his cruiser, to called, for backup, Cain had gone out the back, to catch him, before he could have called for backup. As Cain, had drag the deputy, to the van and put him inside. Cain hit the deputy with a crowbar, pretty hard. Once inside, the van, Cain gave another two hits, on the head. Now the deputy is dead for sure. Now Cain runs into the house, to get the women, and try to dispose the cruiser in the back of, the house. "That was a very close called." Cain, said. "What about the car?" ask, Dana. "I'll put it in, the backyard." said, Cain. "Let's get going! For we be notice." said, Cain. Now as they make it pass, the Bentford's place, Terra, will send, Cain along with Dana, to grab Sam next. But no easy task, now with Sam's brother-in-law in, the picture, it looks like a battle, with veterans versus new school rookies. More of a teachers and students battling, for supremacy, to take over a school building.

Without discipline, regulations and rules. But Ben, Sam's brother-in-law, are great with kids. But doesn't have any of his owned, Benjamin's wife was diagnosed with early dementia, years earlier. With Her health, deteriorating wouldn't allow her, to have any children's. But Benjamin, wanted, to adopt a son, but his work load, was keeping him very busy, for sure. As it starts, to snow Terra and her crew, pass by the Bentford's place, to see if there are changes, to the place. The pickup is in, the driveway, the lights are on in the house. As Cain drives a little slower, to get an ideal, and the layout of, the place and goes and make more plans, with the boss. "Hey I got, a couple of ideals, that may work, for our benefit." said, Cain. "Ok." "Let's hear, them once we get back." said, Terra.

Now riding, with a dead deputy in, the van is, asking, for a lot of, trouble if they ever got pulled over. So, with Cain thinking like a criminal, would think. It's cold and snowing, so Cain dumps, the deputy's body, not far from the Bentford's place, which isn't nothing new around the area. Now that Terra, is very convince of Cain's work ethics, she will reward him of something good. Which her and Dana, thought of getting rid of the men period, and do the job, themselves. But Dana, thought that is a very bad ideal, to do. Dana convinces Terra we need a man power and help in thinking as well. Looks like Cain is spared. Can't say the same for Bobby.

A Moment Before
Chapter III

The Day has come and went, for Terra to carried out her plan, to cause havoc on, the Bentford's. As riding back, to their hideout, Cain had come up, with a couple of, ideals in getting Sam. Therefore, Terra already knows, that Sam's health isn't the greatest, but he is, the weakest link, that she could pick. So, if an unlucky Sam is alone somewhere, could be an opportunity, for Terra and crew, And Sam a sitting duck.

"So, we could have lured, him out of, the house, by telling him, that we need, for him, to come in, for a new insurance policy. "Said, Cain. "Then I would, steal a car, from somewhere else, to use to cause, an accident, with him inside." said, Cain. "But what if, Jon or Sheila is with him, then what?" ask, Terra. "I think, that we ought, to grab, them as well." said, Cain. "Ok, I'm for that, but it better work!" said, Terra. As both Cain and Dana, stood there looking and listening, to Terra. They notice, that one of, her eyes, has change colors, in which, may her look, a little spook. "Terra! Your eye! Looks greener, then usual." said, Dana. "Wow! How in, the world, you do that?" ask, Cain. "Just something, I inherited, from my father's side." said, Terra. "Would you both, stop looking at me. Please!" said,

Terra. So, when are you, getting another car, for to do, the job?" ask, Terra. "Oh, anymore suggestions?" ask, Terra. "Yes! The time to get him, to come and sign, his life away?" ask, Dana. While everyone was laughing, as a joke. Meanwhile in a couple of days, Sam and family, would see his brother-in-law, arrive at, the Lajunta Airport, to welcome him. As Sheila, doing her best, to keep, the house, immaculate condition, for her uncle's stay. As Sheila thought, would be great, if her mother, was here, to see her brother's visit, from Hawaii. June would, be tickle with joy, to see her younger brother, in the flesh. Jon also getting his weapons cleaned up, for to do some hunting in, the coming spring. As Jon, goes through, his closet, he comes up on his old bowling shoes, he forgot, that he had. So, Jon pulls, them out, to see if he could still fit them, and he can. So, he could accompany, his uncle, to a game of, bowling. Sam use, to bowl, when him and June, had gotten together in, the earlier years. But started, to have issues in holding, the ball, with carpal tunnel, really bad in his right wrist. Then his knees and hip, from arthritis sat in. But on a good night, June herself, could get a perfect 300. without any distraction. Jon couldn't bowl, to save his soul, but he tried, his best, to bowl gutter balls instead. Now Sheila, is like her mother, with a hand on a goodnight. If she concentrated enough. Now there's Benjamin, who is an excellent bowler, who can teach a few tricks in holding, a ball, a moment before, let the ball go, to give it that curve, for the main pin. On Wednesday nights, a family can bowl, for half price and get the bar included, for happy hour. All of this after 4pm. The Bentford's could use, a little excitement, right about now, for all that has been, to them.

Benjamin's stay could, livened things up. Just Benjamin alone, could be a very extraordinary presence, to a positive way, of living. Just having a former detective around is also a great thing. It sounds like, the Bentford's are excited, that, June's younger brother is staying, for a while. Jon and Sam, are discussing if Benjamin, could have Jon's room, to stay in. And Jon, was very delighted in letting his uncle, have his room. As both Sam and Jon, standing in, the doorway of Jon's bedroom, there they heard, a locomotive, with a loud horn on it, pulling other 5 locomotives behind it. Sam and Jon, went into, the kitchen, to the back door, to see what will happen. The train, just kept on going, then Sam and Jon, turns and looks, at one another and starts laughing. "Son! What in, the world, are we doing?" ask, Sam. "I really, don't know." said Jon. Minutes later, here comes Sheila, with her eyes, like a baby doe, when headlight is on it. "What's funny! You guys?" ask, Sheila. Then she started, to laugh about, the situation. Now back at, the hideout. Cain told, Terra, that he needs, to go to a nearby pay phone, to call in a favor, from a guy, he grew up with. This guy, has his own chopped shop, with any car that was stolen, from nearby cities. The guy is Nuel Reyes, a man, with a plan, to get your car. And Nuel is also a loan shark, that has a harsh interest rate, on the money he lends, to people, if not paid back, he will take your vehicle instead. Cain is making, Terra's plans solid, to be very accurate. So that stolen car is, a small diversion, to get Sam or all of them. But before, Cain leaves, he disposes, the dead deputy body where he dumps, Bobby's corpse. Now the facility, is reeking very badly, with two dead corpses inside. And the smell is, driving, the ladies nuts. "Cain!! you have to, do something about this smell, it's gross in here!" said, Terra. "I agree." said, Dana. "Sorry Terra, those guys, are in a septic tank, and I don't know, how far down, that tank goes." said, Cain. "Hey it was alright in here, until you started dumping, dead guys, so please! No more dumping." said, Terra. "Ok boss." said, Cain. "Well, I'm taking off, to the pay phone, I be back, shortly." said, Cain. "Cain one more thing, see if your guy, can drive, the car, to us." said, Dana. "I see if he can" said, Cain. "Cain! Thanks for everything" said, Terra. As Cain was leaving, the women, heard a lot of noise, near and around, the side of, the facility. But can't place, the noise, so both women, with guns, goes and check it out. "Oh, my Goodness! Those look like sewer rats, with babies! "said, Dana. "Sh--! We got dead men in here, and f—king rats too!!?" ask, Terra. "Damn it!" said Terra. "Tee! What are we going, to do?" ask, Dana. "We might, need to relocate." said, Terra.

While the women, tried to stay out of the way of, the rodents and endurance, the smell of, the dead men and sewage water, and getting ready, to have company. What else, can go wrong? As Cain reported back, to the hideout, to deal with two women, and their attitudes. To Cain, it's starts, to become sickening. But he would, put up with it, for a little season. Until he makes, his move. Because, Cain believe, that soon or later, he knows, Terra will get rid of, him also. Without a shadow of doubt, it's coming. So, he is prepared, to move on.

"Hey I'm back!" said, Cain. As the women runs, to Cain, for him to do something, about the rodents. "Whoa! Where, did those come from?" ask, Cain. "Man! Please! Do something!" said, Dana. "What I'm I going to do? Tell them, to get out?" said, Cain. But Cain, needed, some light, to see what's going on, and saw that there was, a family of; possums. So, it looks, like they, were there first in, the building. Cain did, the unthinkable, he found, an old pipe, and beat like it's no one business. He killed a mother and two of her babies. Then he cleaned up, his mess, by throwing them outside of the building, for bird chow.

"Hey let's leave, for a while, to catch some fresh air, how about that?" ask, Cain. So, him and the women, took a ride, As Terra, suggested, to ride by, the Bentford's, see what's happening there. As getting close, to the house, Terra and crew, can see, that the Bentford's, are leaving, to go somewhere, So Cain, can slowly follow them, to their destination. Without being notice, Because, sooner or later, they will notice, they are being followed. So, Cain, has followed, the family, to a plaza, that has a grocery store, more like a shopping center, with a huge bowling alley. They watch, the Bentford's, ever move, as they walk into, the bowling alley. Then Terra, sends both Cain and Dana in, to see what's happening, as she stayed put. Because, Terra, and crew, are wanted, and if Terra, goes into, the building, the family would recognize, who she is right away. Then a fight, may break out, between Terra, Dana and Sheila. Terra and Sheila, never did like each other Because, they both are goodly, to look upon. Sheila is beautiful, without a smile, that how gorgeous, she can be. Terra on the other hand is, also gorgeous, but evil rules, her and no good, can change her. What a way, to adjust too. They both, are alike, accept one knows, how to love, and the other, only knows evil and hate.

Once the Bentford's got inside, they were at the counter, getting lots of information, for as prices on shoes and mainly discounts on what nights, to appear, for happy hour. As they were getting information on everything. Cain and Dana were standing there, getting all the information themselves. But Cain, was gazing, at Sheila, with thoughts, naughty thoughts as he gets his eyes full, of Sheila's body. And knows, this what got Bobby, killed. "Wow baby, I wish, I had you, for a night." Cain's thought. Not only him, being bad, Dana is eyeing Jon's back side, wishing she can just bump into his butt, and hold it. Dana's thought. Because, Jon wears his, jeans a little tight, to fit. And that why Dana is gazing a little harder. Now that both Cain and Dana, got their eyes, full and heads with naughty thoughts, they have, the information on making everything right, on getting Sam Bentford, for Terra's prisoner. But Cain will keep his thoughts, to himself, Cain likes Sheila, but never would he tell, his boss that. And Dana likes Jon, but she can't tell, Terra that, for her to throw a tirade. See how a beautiful someone, can change a person, that doesn't know how, to love, and do good, with also respect, for others. Sheila can change Cain and Jon can do, the same with Dana. But if Terra knows, about her crew doing, and having thoughts, of leaving her and doing good, with showing care, for the Bentford's in anyway, she could kill, them both. So, both Cain and Dana, needs, to be very careful, around their boss. Again, at a drop, of a hat, Terra could kill, without them knowing, she getting ready, to execute. As leaving, the bowling alley, Dana did the unthinkable, by walking into Jon's backside "Oh Sorry sir," said, Dana. "No pardon me," said, Jon. But Jon checked, to see if his wallet, was still in his back pocket, and it was. Cain needed, one more look at Sheila's body, before leaving, to report back, to Terra. As both Cain and Dana, walks back, to the van, keeping Terra, from certain, things. But give her, the information, she is looking, for no more, no less. "What took you both, so long?" ask, Terra. "I started, to think, they caught, you both in there." said Terra. "Well, we got all, the information, we need," said, Cain. "Oh Yeah. Let's hear it" said, Terra. "They are signing up, for someone, that is coming, to visit them," said Dana. "Oh, but it doesn't change a thing." said, Terra. "I still, want, that old bastard, I will not, give up, until I get'em!!" said, Terra. As Cain looks, at Dana, with a serious face, and Dana, did the same.

Now that, the crew starts, to show feeling, for Terra's enemies, that they may get, the idea of, turning on her. Sometimes it's hard, to find loyal friends anymore, unless they are in your pocket, or maybe getting something out of, the deal. The big problem is, they thought, they knew, Terra well. But Terra's house, she built, may become divide, soon or later. As the Bentford's, were coming out of, the bowling alley headed, to their truck. When Terra, notice them, from her eyes, her hair on her head, her nails and hands, all changed. The parasite, started, to transgress in front of her crew. "Terra! What in the world!!" said, Dana. Cain gets out of, the van when he, saw what was going on. "Cain! Get back here!" said, Terra. It took Cain a moment, to get back into, the van. While Terra, goes back normal. But on the way, back to, the hideout, no one said a word. Because, the crew, needs some answers. "I'm sorry both you, I know, you both are wandering, what just happen" said, Terra. "Terra! You were something else, a new side, we never, thought, to see!" shucks!" said, Cain. "So, is, that something you inherited, from your father?" ask, Dana. "I'm afraid, so." said, Terra. Now Terra's crew, are in deep thought, about everything. Cain, needs more, then what Terra is telling them. And Dana, is having second, thoughts on everything she has seen, but has thought on taking out, her boss herself. So, both, Cain and Dana can be very vulnerable, to Terra in murdering them. Once back at, the hideout, they sat down, discussing, the plans in getting Sam. But no one was in a talkable mood. Because, the crew is, still shock, at what they saw in, the van. Terra never told, them anything about a gift, she received, during birth, and for one, she didn't know, she had it, at first. Until one night, she discovers, her eyes were different colors, her hair grew a little long, then normal. It's an evil gift, that she inherited, from her old man's sake. A gene, that she can't get rid of, unless she died, then it's gone for good. Dana has a question, for Terra. "What about, Jon, you mention before," said, Dana. "I had him, believing, that I was pregnant, by him, for him and his father, to fight each other; I had, them both playing them against the other, to divide, their house." said, Terra. "That why, I need, for you both, to help kill, this family off. For my father death. "The moment, before we kill him, I would like, to torment him, like he did me," said, Terra. "Ok, I'm so ready, to do this, for sure." said, Dana. As those words, was said, to put a smile on, the boss's face. To do evil, of course, that's what's make, the devil even happy. In darkness, all dirty evil deeds are done. Cain! Are you in!? "ask, Terra. "Let's do it." said, Cain. But in Cain's head, he can't wait, to see Sheila, again. To keep her out of harm's way. Now Dana is, have thoughts about having her and Jon, to hook up in a way, that she can be held like a woman, wants, to be held. Cain is thinking deeply, about getting out, and turn himself in, to be with a woman like Ms. Sheila. Cain thinks, that a woman like Sheila, can change a man like him into a great person. Cain wants, to do good, Cain wants, to learned, to do good and to love as well. As a knocked, at the door, everyone had pulled, their piece, for any static, from, the cops, But it was Nuel Reyes, with a stolen vehicle, for the kidnapping of Sam. As Nuel, walks in, he looks, at Terra, like he knew, her back in the day. "Hey, don't I know, your woman?" ask, Nuel. "I don't think, so." said, Terra, with a sassy stance and a dirty look. That minute, turned, Nuel on. "I like you, already!" said, Nuel.

Death at First Sight
Chapter IV

As Cain and Nuel, walks out, to check, the car out, Cain told, Nuel, to be careful, trying, to pet on a lioness, because, he may get bit, for standing to close. So, a polite warning, was given. Now Nuel, can go on his own risk. "I like this car, Noel. "said Cain. "I'm willing, to let you have it, if I can have all girl in there, just for a little while." Nuel, said. "Which one are you, talking about?" Cain, ask. "The one, with the beautiful butt on her." Nuel, said. "Hey Man! I warn you, but be my guest." Cain, said. "All man, she can't be all that bad, and the way it looks, I can teach, her a few tricks, if she is willing, to learn." Nuel, said. "Man, you just don't understand." Cain, said. "Go and be my guest, for some people, don't want, to listen." Cain said. As going back into, the dungeon of a building, Nuel steps, to Terra, to see if he can talk, to her in private about getting, to know her, a little better. But with a heed warning, from his friend, he should've taken. First thing is first, Nuel show up uninvited, he seen everyone's face, that is, Terra's and Dana's in which don't look upon them. Because, both women can be very deadly, when working together. So don't play with water, near electricity. That what Cain, was trying, to tell Nuel. "So, what are you, doing later?" Nuel, ask. With an evil stare, Terra, wants, to kill him, but not right now. "Why? And this, better be about, that raggedy car, you brought over here!" Terra, said. And with both, women standing there, like two she bears, that wants, to tear into, their prey, and eat. And Nuel looks helpless, just standing there, with his tail between, his legs. "What you, going, to take us both out?" Terra, ask. "Whoa I meant you, and you alone." Nuel, said. "IF you want me, she has, to come too." Terra, said. "Well ok. Shucks!" Nuel, said. "What's a matter, you can't handle two women alone?" Dana, said. Now Cain knew, that this was going, to occur, to his good friend, from back in, the day. He knows, that Nuel is already dead, from the looks of things. But Nuel, did insist on, messing, with Terra. And not knowing, that she is very dangerous, to bother with. As much as possible, Cain wanted, to stop everything, but if he does, Terra would kill him, alone with his buddy. So as both women getting ready, to commit another homicide on another man, for being nosey, showing up uninvited, the identity he can provide, for the cops and messing with, the wrong women. But Cain, wishes he can talk Nuel out of doing, this, but his mind is, so on Terra's butt, it's too late. "Hey Cain! The car is yours." Nuel, said. As leaving, both women looking at Cain, the same way, they gave Bobby, that look, that your time is up. With two bullets a piece into, their victims. But Cain knows, to keep his mouth shut, and let things, take its course. The women, are in charge, and don't resist them, what man is going, to resist a well fashion curvy woman, with a beautiful face and can smile, from here, to the Grand Canyon. Now everything is set, to put Nuel, to sleep permanent, for what he did, has compromised, their operation. So, Terra can't have Nuel, go run and tell, the authorities anything. Once he is deceased, he doesn't know a thing. He can't help.

"So where are, you taking us?" Terra, ask. "I would like, to take you both, to eat, then my place, how about that?" Nuel, ask. "Ok, Cool." said, Terra. They all, climb into Nuel's truck, to head, to a restaurant, to eat. Because, both ladies, hasn't had a decent meal, since, they being on, the run. "I have a great ideal, why don't you, grab, the food, and take it back, to your place?" Dana, ask. "The women know, that they would be at risk, sitting out in a diner, full of people, that can identify them, being with Nuel. "We can, do that too." Nuel, said. As Nuel, was driving, Terra was staring at him, like he did something wrong, to her, but she was just admiring, the guy, for taking interested, in her. But business is business and she, has, to closed, the curtains on a sweet guy like Nuel. The diner, that they drive, to is a cousin, to Nuel, that owned the establishment, and his name is, Miguel Reyes, who loves cooking, for the local community. Nuel and Miguel are like brothers growing up, in the Rio Grand area, with their grandmother raising them both. But the real crazy, thing Nuel did, was introduce, both women, to his cousin Miguel, which was a very awful ideal, for to kill Nuel, for sure. Now that, the women have been exposed, it calls, for more murders, then usual. As Nuel and Miguel, walks back, to the building, the women, are really upset, with Nuel's way of doing things. So, Dana, wants, to put a bullet in his temple, for the damage he is causing. But once, back at his place, its curtains, for him. Then somehow, the women, are contemplating, to come and get the cousin as well. The women's thoughts, are that the law is still, looking, for them. And it puts, them further in trouble, with law enforcement. "Can you believe, this s.o.b, we don't need any attention, from nobody." Terra, said. "He is really going, to get it." Dana, said. As a man does, is tell his brother, buddies, cousins, road dogs all males, that they got it like that, with two fine, women with him. To him, it's a big deal, to the females, it's about clowning, to death. "Terra and Dana knows, that Nuel is showing off, with the two of, them with him.

But the women, are itching, to correct, the matter once, they get to his place. "So how should, we do this, by eating first, then do him in?" Dana, asked. "I suppose, we can do that, I really wish, this guy would c'mon!" Terra, said. While sitting in, the truck, a Sheriff deputy, pulls up next to, the truck, to go in and order, takeout. But when he got out of, the cruiser, the deputy spoke, to both women. "Howdy." said, the deputy. As both women, had their weapons, half way concealed, for easy access. "Oh Shucks. What in the f@#%& are, we going, to do now?" Dana, asked. "Nuel! Is a dead man, for sure now." said, Terra.

Now that Nuel, had to wait on, the food, to cook thoroughly, the women, are blaming him, for everything. The guy, wants, to be, with

Terra. But she, wants, to kill him, for putting them in jeopardy, with a deputy, parked on the other side of them. Now that Nuel is coming, with the food, his ears are about, to get a cussing out, by both women, for everything he has done wrong. But Nuel, has an evil, temper as well. Nuel isn't a push over, in what the ladies, may think. "Nuel! You muthaf#%@! We didn't need, to meet your ugly ass cousin, and we are hungry man! What you brought us, here, to starve us?" Terra, asked. "Hey!! both of you, bitches, can slow your role!! I had to make sure, that your food was done right sh--!" Nuel, said. "Man! When I was locked up, I was still, blamed, for stuff, that I didn't know about." said, Nuel. "Wait a minute!, you of all people, was lockup?" Terra, asked. "Hell yeah! I was lockup, for 12 years, for I accidentally killed a man. But my lawyer, tried, to get me less time. But the judge, saw otherwise." Nuel, said. Both women, just looked at one another, as both women are thinking, that they could abort their mission in committing a homicide. "Nuel, we owe, you an apology." said Dana. While Terra, just staring at the man, while he is driving and it kinda, turned both women into little girls, by listening, to him, talk to them, like that. The question is, Did Terra, found her man, or her victim still? Because, she, is known, to be unpredictable, like the weather on some days. But whatever she is thinking, it's not good. Now that Cain, is by himself, he thought of, taking, the van to look upon, Sheila, of course, with a small of a crush on a beautiful young and tender woman, but also bitter, when it comes to the family, and mainly her father. Because, she is still, daddy's girl. If Cain, do this, he must be very, discreet in going, over, to the Bentford's place. Cain could've learned, from Bobby 'screw up, on the first day of, scope, the family house. And got caught. But Cain, is a thinker, and sort of street smarts. As he is thinking, on how to get Sheila, out of, the house, to hold a conversation, with her. "I know, what to do now." Cain, thinking out loud. Cain goes and get into the van, and start driving, to see another buddy of his, to get a few bucks, from him. He goes to see Lucas Hamm, who runs a flower stand at a mall nearby. Cain pulls up, to where Lucas, can see him coming. "Hey Luc! What's shaken, beside the baken?" "Hey CoCain, you're a wanted, and do me, a favor, stay, the heck, away, from me." said Lucas. "Man, I just want to know, if I could, get five dollars, from you, and a couple of roses. Please?" Cain, asked. "Sure. But get, the hell out of here man." Lucas, said. Lucas, use, to bend backwards, for Cain. Until he beat a guy senseless, for asking Cain, to buy him a beer, and when Cain, refuses, the guy spit on Cain. And then Cain, grab, the nearest pipe, and laid, that guy out and left him, for dead.

Now that Cain, has the tools, to go and see, this lovely woman as he gets closer, to her house, his adrenaline is working, that his heart rate, just speed up, that Cain, thought he is having a heart attack or something. "I got, to get it, together." Cain, said. "She is just a woman, a fine woman at that." Cain, said. Cain has made it, there as he parks, the van down, the road, to walk, to asked, to use, their phone, to have someone, to come and look, at the van. Cain walks up, the porch, and knock on, the door. And his adrenaline, really got, the best of him and Sheila answer, the door. "Hi can I help you?" Sheila, asked. "Hi my van stop on me, can I use, your phone?" Cain, asked. "Well, my father, could, take a look at it, he's a mechanic, if you like?" Sheila, ask. As Cain, stood there, trying, to say something, as he watches Sheila's lips move. More like he was in a trance in sleeping and walking at the same time. Sheila came outside, to talk with him, but Cain's lips wasn't moving, for some reason. "Hey man, are you ok?" Sheila, asked. "Oh yeah, I'm just cold, that's all. "Cain, said. "Where are you parked?" Sheila, asked. "Down next, to the corn-field." Cain, said. "Excuse me, What's your name?" Cain, asked. "Sheila." said, Sheila. "And yours?" Sheila, asked. "Cain." said, Cain. "Let me, see if I can start it again." Cain, said. "Can I walk, with you?" Sheila, asked. "Wow, you sure can." Cain, said. As Cain, thought, it works. The next, thought, is making Sheila, his main girl. But he knows, he has to crawl, before he walks, but still, things, with him, and Terra and Dana, would really go sour, and deadlier.

But Cain, knows, that he has, to sacrifice something, to be with Sheila, and that is, to kill off, Dana. Because, if Dana is around, when going up against, Terra. Then Dana, would make a counter attack, on him. To make, things right, for the boss. So, he knows, to take out Dana, before Terra. Besides, Terra is nothing, without Dana. As a pair of, women on, the run, they now are known, as Thelma and Louise. Cain, thought. As both Cain and Sheila, had made it, to the van. Cain gets in, to start up, the van, and it started right up. "Well, it started up." said, Cain. "Maybe it needed, to sit, for a minute, before starting it again." Sheila, said. As both, just stared one another in, the eyes, and Sheila notice, the two roses in, the passenger seat, "Wow, who's those for, your girlfriend? "asked, Sheila. "No, these, are for a special lady, you are that lady." said, Cain. The minute, Cain told, her that, Sheila didn't know, what to say, or how, to act. "Thank you, Cain, you are mighty thoughtful." said, Sheila. "Sheila! Can, I see you again, please?" ask, Cain. "Well let me think, on that ok?" asked, Sheila. "I can, live, with that." said, Cain. "I'll see you again." Sheila, said. "Well Sheila, you have a great evening." Cain, said. Then Cain, drove on. As he tried, to get back, before, the rest of, the group does. Now Cain, planet, a seed between himself and Sheila. In which, he has, to be careful, he has, to figure, a way to come clean, by turning everybody in, to the cops, or just himself. Either way, he has, to work very fast, unless, those women, put, the drop on him first. If Terra ever, found out, what Cain has done, or what's he is up, to. He ain't got, to worried, about seeing, Sheila. Sheila will see him in, the obituary section of, the newspaper. That's the ruthless of Terra. So now he can't, follow through, with Terra's orders, to ruin this family. So everything, that Terra wanted done. Cain, absolutely will go against, the grain, for this family, even putting his life in danger, for Sheila. Cain's crush, for Sheila, has turned, to love and respect. And so a house divided, will not stand together. Like they say, evil is for evil, and good is for good. But often, to see evil and good, to work together no way. Now that Nuel, and the women are at his place eating, Terra has decided, to go back on her word, to kill Nuel, for exposing, them, to his cousin and had them waiting awhile in the truck, starving, with a Sheriff deputy parked next, to the truck. So with all of that, Terra takes offense, to all of that. Why? Because, Terra can, whenever and whatsoever she the Boss of this outfit, and do what she is well please, to do. But to Cain, there is another boss, to him, her name is Sheila. So Cain is willing, to pledge an allegiance, to Sheila, and commit a mile of treason, under Terra's leadership. And Nuel, who is, trying, to be part of, the Terra's regimes, by breaking bread, with her and her protégé. But Terra, wants, to kill him still. It's part of her nature. Just like a scorpion, you can poke scare it, play with it, it's still going, to sting you, because of its nature, to do that. If all of God's, creation had a conscience, it wouldn't be so bad, to play with a snake, scorpion, even a lion and a bear. But between, that and Terra, she has a conscience, to think and tried, to do good. But part of her conscience is shared, with this evil parasite.

As Nuel, sat and talk, with Dana and Terra, about a trip, to his country New Mexico. But Terra has to use, the bathroom, this is her cue, to get ready, to do a homicide. By going, to the Bathroom, but she doesn't, she is in another part of the house. To get you or whoever, to come and look, for her. And now they are a victim. But Nuel, is very smart, by holding a conversation with Dana, until Terra will return. But Terra needs, to get Nuel, to his bedroom, for her plan, to work. Nuel is absolutely not holding up, Terra's game. Now Dana is, going, to persuade Nuel in going, to check up on Terra. But he still insists, that she can, find her way back, to them in the kitchen. "I think, she wants you, to come and see her in your bedroom, I believe." said, Dana. "Ok well I guess, I need, to go and see her." said, Nuel. But if he goes, to his room, there death waiting on him. "Terra! What's up baby?" asked, Nuel. And walking, to his bedroom, though, the door, Terra is standing behind his door, to give him something. "There you are, my friend!" said, Nuel. Terra grab him, before she shoots him, "I wanted, to give you this. She kissed, him. (Pow!). As she stood over him, while he fights, to breathe. Terra and Dana, grab what they can and split, by taking Nuel's truck. And Dana, goes, to Nuel to get what's in his pockets, and Nuel was still fighting, for air. But Dana, didn't care, she only wanted, a free dinner and what's in his pockets. As Terra waits outside, for Dana, Because, Dana is the one that's driving. But little, the women know, that Nuel, was shot in, the shoulder, near his neck. After, the women were gone, he hobbles, to the phone, to call paramedics, to come. While he lay still, until they arrived. Now Nuel's thoughts, are after this, it's about to get real ugly, with these women. But only, if he survives, with the blood, he has already lost. Now the women are on, their way back, to the hideout, And now the crew, needs a new location right about now, After that stunt, Nuel will come looking, for them, with his crew of buddies. They took Nuel's kindness, for weakness. That hurts Nuel's intelligence, and damage his pride, with his manhood step on. Nuel's thoughts, Give a woman a complement, and she screams, sexual assault, you take a lady out, she tried, to kill you. What in the name of God, is this world coming too? Now the paramedics have arrived, as Nuel open, the front door, to go outside, to his front porch, to get into the ambulance, but he collapsed, on his front porch. But paramedics quickly, rolls, the gurney, to get Nuel up off, the ground. "It's looks like he already lost a lot of blood." said, a medic. While the other medic, put a ventilator on him, to help him, to breathe. As the medics, checks Nuel's vitals before getting him, to the hospital. "Hey sir! Would you like, to tell us, what happen here?" asked one medic. "A couple of bit—es. That's what happened." Nuel, said. As the medics laughing, at the sense of humour, that Nuel display. That means, he is going, to be alright. "Hey bud, we need, for you, to lay still." said, the medic. And as Nuel, lay still until they get to the hospital, Nuel has all kind of crazy thoughts, going through, his head. But one is, that he will deal, with those women later, after his hospital stay. Nuel thought, two was no women, going, to shoot me, and get away, with it. Nuel, thought.

As Dana and Terra, driving back, to the hideout, they both are sitting, laughing, and bragging about, what just happened. And little, they know, that Nuel will be ok. Now revenge seeks revenge. So Terra, now has an enemy, that's on her path. Now both, women arrived, at the hideout. As they both quickly moves, to get inside, to see Cain. And let him know, what had transpired. But Cain, started, to argued, with both women, for what they had done. "Nuel was a good man, and you both destroyed him!" said, Cain. "For what!!?" asked, Cain. Both women, pulled their guns, on Cain. As one's gun on his head and then the other, she had her gun on his chest, to blow Cain, away. "Are you backing, out Cain!?" asked, Terra. "Look! Ain't no one, talking about, backing out!" said, Cain. "I'm talking about you, two on a passion, for homicides!" said, Cain. "Did you both, make sure, that he was dead!?" asked, Cain.

Both women, just looked at each other. "I when and took, five hundred bucks, off of him." said, Dana. "Dana! That damn money, isn't going, to keep Nuel's henchmens, from killing us!" said, Cain. "I know, we both f*&%# up!, but he did everything in exposing us, to his cousin, then a Sheriff deputy got a look, at our faces, if he can remember them. So we had, to get rid of, him!!" said, Terra. "Terra! that man, really did like you, that's all he talked about, that night, when he first saw you standing there." said, Cain. "Ladies please! Think, before, you shoot someone." said, Cain. Then Terra walks over to Cain, by getting in his face. "Cain, are you, going soft on us?" asked, Terra. "Because, if I even, think of you going soft and changing, it's game over, for you, and last time, I check, I was the boss of, this union." said, Terra.

Now in Cain's head, he knows, what he must do, to dethrone this bitch and her protégé too. "Terra, you are absolutely, the boss." said, Cain. Then he walks over, to the doors, to see if any signs of, authorities, but sees no one. Cain's thought, of being, with Sheila right about now, is better being, with these two rogue individuals on any giving day. "Cain! I think it's time, for us to relocate, any suggestions?" asked, Terra. "Well didn't, your father, have an old shack, not far off, from the Bentford's place?" asked, Cain. "Wait a minute, your right, I did, mention that. Because, that is where he was trying, to kill Sheila's ass." said, Terra.

"Well we can, go by there, tomorrow, if we have time." said, Cain. Cain thought, you're the boss, but keep looking, to me, for answers. As this crew of, Terra's is soon, to disintegrate, quickly. Because, of the leadership has no stern guideness about it, with a young woman, that has hated to do good, to make good, that is in charge. With no experience, whatsoever. But she will run, to confide into Cain but she is, the one, that calls all, the shots. How is it, that the so-called boss can make a small mistake? And have the so called, little people, to clean it up. But Cain is about, to do the unthinkable, thing by going clean, and turning himself in to the authorities. For in order, to be or see Sheila again, he must sacrifice his career in, doing wrong.

Now both women, must have been, talking, with one another, Because, Terra has Dana, watching Cain closely on his every move. Every time, Cain would look up, Dana would, just give him an evil eye, like she, can just shoot him, and be done with it. So the tension is, starting, to build, where everything starting, to unreveal apart. Cain knows, that Terra must know, something else, that got her all work up. She and Dana, kill a guy, for nothing, because, things weren't going, their way exactly. And that, could have her, so on edge. But is thinking that she would have, to go, to her inter being, to kill all of Nuel's guys and Nuel too. Understanding that Terra, didn't want a guy, too close, to her, excepted Dana. Because, Terra's situation, with her parasite inside, will not let a man, do anything, to her. So how can you, get a woman work up, with a strong and strange creature, coming out of, her? Nuel, kissing Terra, and suddenly, her arms and legs, got hairy and eyes are different colors. It would, causes a lot of questions, for the man, and Terra would have some answers on what happened.

Familiar Face

Chapter V

As winter weather put a damper on, tomorrows hunt, for to relocate, from, the abandon steam plant, to Terra's father's old shack, that's near, the Bentford's home. And as, the snow falls in those parts of the region, they can be snow in, for a couple of days. And Cain, isn't liking, that to well, by being in secluded, with a couple of women bandits. Cain, thoughts. If getting away, from them two, to be with Sheila, he would come, to an excuse, to leave. On a snowy day, like this. Benjamin's flight landed safe, from Hawaii, to Lajunta airport. Once inside, the terminal, he walks to a pay phone, to call Sam, to let him know, that he arrived safe and sound. Now Benjamin's luggage is, needed, to be claimed, through security check. So it would, take a minute. "Hey Sammy! I'm here, at the airport, I see you guys getting a lot of snow. Wow!" said, Benjamin. "Just letting you know, that imam here. ok." said, Benjamin. Sam is so relief, that his brother-in-law, has made it safe, through the bad weather, that they are receiving.

Therefore, the micro problem is, to go and get him, in a foot of snow, that fell, in an hour and a half. The truck, has no rear wheel power. But understand, this is a 1978 Ford F150 big boy. So Jon, would have, to put sand bags in, the bed of, the truck, to give it, that weight, for traction. Now Sheila's 1979 Chevy Monte Carlo, can also handle, the snow. But Sheila, isn't going anywhere, without her dad and brother. And too, Sheila, doesn't like driving in, the snow, like June, her mom never like driving in bad weather. But Sam doesn't mind, the bad weather, also Jon, is like his old man. Sam told, Jon and Sheila, both about driving in, the bad weather, it makes you stronger, and better at driving too. As Sam and his kids, gather into, the truck, to go and get Benjamin, from the airport. Which they all are excited, to see him, and ready for a home full of laughter and smiles, for days, with him here. Sam is very excited, to have company, by June's older brother, who took a liken, to Samwell being, when they were kids, Ben, also picked on Ed. Ben thought, that Ed, was to nerdy and goofy, for June, to be his girlfriend, but out of, respect, for June, being, his sister, Ben left Ed alone.

But when, Sam shows up, Benjamin was glad, to see his sister with someone, that has a pair and kept, his sister, laughing, with joy. And Ed, couldn't handle that, So June ended up in the arms of, Sam. But June told, Ed, she would still be his friend, but Ed didn't, want June, for a friend, he needed, her for a girlfriend or nothing at all. Then Ed, turned, to the dark side of things. On certain, occasions, it burned Ed up inside, to see both Sam and June, together and then when, the couple had their first child together, Ed really couldn't take at all. Because, Ed, always thought, that June would have a baby with him, instead of Sam. So with all, that Ed had bottle all his hate, for this couple, for years and years. When Ed, found out that, Sam and June, had a second child, the man lost it completely. And he is why June isn't, with her family. So if he couldn't have her, Sam couldn't have her neither. Evil, evil, evil and evil. Benjamin, would be thrilled, to see his sister in, the flesh and Sam and her accomplishments. And Ben, will want some answers, about his sister's death and who did it. But once, he knew, who did it, he would use his experience as a former detective and catch, the guy. But he would've found out, that his dear nephew, took, the guy out, for good sake. Ben is looking, to have a great time, with his family, without a shadow of doubt. And with a New Year ahead, Ben even thought, of looking, for some part time work, with one of, the surrounding law agency, to keep his experience sharp. But he rather, take it easy, then to chase, criminals back and forth.

But in Ben's mind, he would love, to do it all over again, if his body would allow him, to do it. It's just the excitement being a cop, going after criminals. And solving a crime, was his forte. In Ben's career, he has solved over 200 crimes and 60 he couldn't clear, and 140 arrest. So Benjamin was great at what he does best. But one case, he arrested, a crook, for a B/E, but the judge, threw it out, because, it was, the prosecutor's cousin, that did, the crime. So the Prosecutor, had, the Judge, to throw, the case out that burnt, Benjamin's reputation a bit. Ben didn't care, for the system, at times, because, it will favor, the scum bag, at times, Ben would, work hard, to catching, a criminal, and the courts, shows favor in the criminal, and he or she gets, to go home, and Ben and the rest of, the force, doesn't know, what to think. So time after time, Ben and his fellow detectives goes, and make an arrested, and the Prosecutors and Judges, working with, the criminals. That is corruption, for miles under a table bribery. For Cops and Detectives, to look, the other way. But Benjamin, wouldn't take a darn dollar, from no one. He was there, to uphold, the law and no amount of, money couldn't stop him, from doing his job. At one point, it was hard, to work, with Ben, because, of his partners, would take bribes, and he wouldn't, so that would, let you know, who was on, the take, and who wasn't.

Ben can have recalled, when one of, his partners in previous years, was sent to prison, for corruption, to kill Benjamin, for a known, gangster. But Ben had found out on, the streets, that his so-called partner is, looking, for ways to take him out, for a ransom of 300,000.00 dollars. So that, the gangster's family member wouldn't do time. This is to keep, Ben, from testifying against the family member.

After all, the gangster's family member had, to do 50 years sentences, and Ben's former ex detective, had a life sentence for counts of bribery and premeditated on a fellow detective. Ben felt very good in, getting scum like that off of, the streets. Thinking, what his ex-partner, is doing by becoming someone's bit-- in, the joint. So Benjamin, love, the job, and care at what he did, and at, the end of, the day, Benjamin knows, he did, the right thing in his heart.

Now that Sam is driving, the roads aren't as bad. With snow, drifting and some spots, are icy. But Sam just, kept on driving, to get his brother-in-law with a bit of excitement. Until Jon, started singing "Oh Danny boy, the pipes, the pipes are calling." Jon, singing. "Excuse you, can you turn, the radio on please?" said, Sheila. "Your singing is, kinda off." said, Sheila. Now being 45 minutes, from the airport, Sam taking his sweet old time, getting his brother-in-law. As passing individuals with their vehicles stuck in the snow, some were stuck on, the side of the road. But getting, closer, to the airport, the roads were salted and clear with some spots, still icy. While sitting at a traffic light, Jon notice, that several, police cruisers went by in a hurried, and it seem like an accident happened, in front of, the airport. "All Sh--!" said, Sam. There was a three-car accident in front of, the airport, to where, they needed, to go in and get Benjamin, with his luggage. But the cops are making everyone detour, from the airport. As Sam, coming up on a cop, he rolls his window down, to speak, with the cop, to see how long is, the entrance way is going, to be down. "Excuse us, how long, is the front of, the airport, going, to be down?" asked Sam. "I say about an hour, because, of cleaning the debris, from, the accident." said, the officer. "ok." said, Sam.

Therefore, there's no other way, to getting onto, the airport grounds, so Sam and family, would have, to wait an hour, before coming, onto the airport. Sam made a suggestion, to go and eat at a nearby diner, to stalled, for time. "But we need, to call Ben and let him know, that we can't get in, to get him, for an hour." said, Sam. "Hey! Reyes is open, we can call him, from there." said, Jon. "Well Reyes! It is." said, Sam. On their way, to this diner, there is a pay phone, outside of the diner. "Does anybody know, the number, to the airport?" asked Jon. So Jon, goes, to Manuel, for a phone book, so he can call, the airport to let his uncle know, that we can pick him up, in an hour. As Jon walks up to the cashier counter and he notice a familiar face. "Hey no fu^#* way." said, Jon. Jon was very surprise, to see a mugshot, of Terra's on the wall, going out, to the pay phone. But before, going outside, Jon went and asked his father and Sheila, to come and look. "What in, the hell, no way." said, Sam. "So she, still at large." said Jon. "Hey Miguel, have you seen her?" Jon, asked. "Her Face, does look all so familiar." said, Miguel. "Wait a minute, since you mentioned it, my cousin, brought two nice looking, women here one-night last week, and one of, the women, looks like her." said, Miguel. "So do you, know, what the other, woman looks like?" asked, Jon. "Not really, because, I was kinda busy though." said, Miguel. "Ok." said, Jon.

I will, called Sheriff Protzman's office tomorrow, to see if anyone is working on, this case" said, Sam "This young bit--! Isn't going, to make our lives miserable. "I said, what I meant, about that whore, if she come, this way, I will kill, that bi---!!" said, Sheila. "C'mon, let's eat, before it's time, to pick up your uncle." said, Sam. "Jonny, go on, and call your uncle" Sam, said. As Jon goes and call, the airport, to get in touch, with Ben, to let him know, that there's an accident in front, of the entrance way in. "Hi I need, to speak with Benjamin Tills, to let him know, that we can't get through, an accident." Jon, said. "Ok, thank you." Jon, said. "Great news, the entrance way is clear." Jon, said. "I have a better ideal, why don't I go get uncle Ben, and bring here, and dad you and Sheila, sit tight." Jon, said. "Son be careful." said, Sam.

Jon got into, the and drove off, like nothing, going and sliding all over, the road. But to Jon, that's fun, to him, doing donuts in, the snow. Jon, just being a boy, for a moment, showing out in, front of patron in, the diner. Suddenly, Miguel is waiting on customer's, he gets a call, from, the hospital, it's about his cousin Nuel, has been shot. "Reyes diner!" said, Miguel. "What! Ok I be there!" said, Miguel. Miguel told, his right-hand man, to lock up, the diner. Right away, Miguel climbs into, his jeep Cherokee, headed, to the hospital, to check up, on what had happened, to his cousin and his best friend. "Man, I hope, he's alright."

Miguel, thought out loud. Once on arrival, at the hospital, Miguel, ran into the emergency entrance, get, the information he needed, for Nuel's status. A nurse, that is treating Nuel's vitals', for blood works, had to come and to comforted Miguel, to let him know, that Nuel is, going to be alright. "Who are you, to the patient?" asked, the nurse. "I'm his cousin, or you can say, more of, a big brother." said, Miguel. "Ok, he is resting, right now, apparently, he has been shot in, the shoulder, just below his neck." said, the nurse. "Can I see him, anytime soon?" asked, Miguel. "Can you, come back, say tomorrow?" asked, the nurse. "Ok, can you, tell him, that Miguel, his cousin was here." said, Miguel. "I will do." said, the nurse.

Meanwhile Jon had made it, to get his uncle, from the airport to returned, to the diner, to get his father and sister. So everyone can be together. "Hey uncle Ben, how are you?" asked, Jon. "Jonny! My nephew! Boy you are all grown up now, and hell, you grown like a weed." said, Ben. "Well I'm good, and it's great, to be with family, I tell you." said, Ben. "Hey I thought, all of, you were coming?" asked, Ben. "We have, to go back, to the diner over, the way, to get Dad and Sheila." said, Jon. "Ok." said, Ben. "Man, is it me, or is it getting colder out here?" asked, Ben. "We you, use to leave here, one point in, time." said, Jon. "And you are, right, I'm just use to that Hawaii warm weather." said, Ben. So as both, men headed back, to the diner, Benjamin was striking up, various talks, about how his sister, was a great person, to be around and how he played pranks on her, like crazy. But it was funny, to him. But her, she would go and, tell on you in a minute. "One day, I was messing, with, that nerdy guy Ed, that if he didn't leave, your mom alone, that I would beat, him up, for a week." said, Ben.

"Uncle Ben, please don't mentioned, that name around, the house, please." said, Jon. "Even though, he's dead, we really, not interested in, that evil man. "Son, I do understand, where you are coming from." said, Ben. As they pulled, up in front of, the diner in deep snow, to get Sam and Sheila, with smiles on everyone's faces. It may be cold and snowing, but happiness is also in, the air. As they saw Benjamin, was an honorable and grateful sight, to see him. As all had, that same thought, that it would, be nice, if June was here, to see her older brother in, the flesh. This family, will always mourn, the death of a great woman, that did excellent things in, the community and her church. June will always be missed, but her legacy will travel, for years, to come.

Instead of leaving, the diner, they all went back inside, to place an order. Benjamin, figured, why go home and mess up, the kitchen, let these, people wait on us. So they grab a booth in, the corner of, the diner. "So how was your flight here?" asked, Sam. "Well it was great, all I thought of, was getting here, to see you all." Ben, said. "It's got, to be crazy, to leave, the warmer climate, to be, with us in cold weather, would you think?" Sheila, asked. "Well my niece! I'm here, babygirl, for, the enjoyment of family." said, Benjamin. "Besides, I need, a break, from the islands and sunny weather, but I do like a bit of variety, at times." said, Benjamin. "Sammy, I know, you don't want me, to mention Ed's name. But I need, to know, myself, what had happened, to my sister?" Ben, asked. "Well the truth is, that June, had went out, that evening, for the church axillary, for the women, to get perishables, for the pantry, but she, never made it back home." said, Sam. "So the authorities, found, June's license plate, to her car on, the railroad tracks, behind, the house. Ed, killed my wife! Your sister! the mother of my two children! So yes we don't want, that name mention in the house!" said, Sam. By Benjamin's thoughts, that Ed could've, live a little longer, for him, to get a hold of him, to kill his butt. Ben knows, that his sister, didn't deserved, to die. But he also knoweth, when the time, for life on earth has ended, you can't avoid it, no kind of way. But June, Ed punched, her time, for her. "Hi my name, Ruthie, I be your server." Ruthie, said. "Hi Ruthie!" said, the Bentford's. "Do you all need a menu?" asked, Ruthie. "Ruthie, let me have, your today's special." said, Ben.

Well, the special is, Pulled Beef, Mac n Cheese with Cabbage and a side of cornbread." said, Ruthie. "Yes let's have that," said, Ben. "Ruthie, we all have, the same." said, Sam. "What are we drinking, today?" Ruthie, asked. "Let us have, sweetteas." said, Sam. "So we still, have a problem, Ed's daughter is still on, the hunt list, and we believe she, is looking for some revenge, for her father's death." Sam, said. "So in other words, she is still, at large?" Ben, asked. "Yup." Sam, said. "At first, we didn't know, that Ed had a daughter, until she had told, us, that she, was his daughter." said, Sam. "She lied, about being pregnant, with Jonny's baby, then tried, to kill, him, in the process, to get me next, but that was all of, Ed's doing." Sam, said. "Poor girl, why didn't, he come after you all himself?" Ben, asked. "He did, with a creature." Jon, said. "Creature!" said, Ben. "What kind of a creature?" Ben, asked. "Ben! We don't know, how he got, that way, but it showed up at the house, on certain occasions though." Sam, said. "So Sammy! How come, you didn't call, the cops?" asked, Ben.

As all three, just looked, at Benjamin, with a looked, that he realized, that you can't tell a police station, that kind of a story for, to be the laughing stock of, the town. With somethings are left unsaid. "So I take it, that you all, took matters in, your own hands?" asked, Ben. "Exactly." Jon, said. "Wow! I see now." said, Ben. "We know, that it took a while, for the Sheriff's office, months, to a year, to get a grip on June's disappearance, then Sheila's whereabouts, was almost longer, then June's absence." said, Sam. "So! Why go, to the authorities, when we can get it done ourselves." said, Sam.

Now that, the snow has lighted up, with some of, the roads being clear, by the city snow removals at work. Miguel, has returned, to his diner, to closed up, for the evening. With some news, that Nuel is, going, to be alright. "How's you folks, doing, is everything ok?" Miguel, asked. "Hey Miguel! How's your cousin holding up?" Jon, asked. "He's holding up, he getting better, from a gunshot wound in his shoulder." said, Miguel. "So what happen?" Jon, asked. "I believed, that this woman, right here, shot him, because, she and another woman was, with my cousin, that night, when he was shot." said, Miguel.

"Uncle Ben! Here is a mugshot, of Ed's daughter. "said, Jon. "O.K. can see, some resemblance in her." said, Ben. "So no one, has found, this woman yet?" Ben, asked. "Obviously not!" said, Jon. "But I believe, she is in on my cousin, getting shot." said, Miguel. "B—ch!" said, Miguel. "Miguel! You are absolutely right, that is what she is." said, Sheila.

"I be, so glad, when, they catch, her stupid ass, before I do, because, I will try, my best, to kill her ass." said, Sheila. "My dear, and lovable niece, please, don't say that. Let the Sheriff do his job. Ok." said, Ben. "Uncle Ben, you just don't understand, this b—ch! Father, tried, to kill me, after he seduce me, so can you see why, I don't like, this woman?" Sheila, asked. "I do understand dear, really I do." said, Ben. "That heifer, wet my sofa, on purpose, because, I knock her ass out, then I tied, her up, to keep her off of me, because, she was trying, to kill me also." said, Sam. "It seems, to me, that this young woman, is very ruthless, at getting, to know people." said, Ben. "I wish, I've could've got here, before all of, this took place." said, Ben.

"Ben, no need, we can handle, this situation, like sweeping a floor, thing is sticking, together like family suppose too." said, Sam. "Here comes, the food, let's eat." Said, Jon. Now that the family had told Benjamin, quite a bit, for heads up on certain things. But Benjamin's thoughts, are to use his skills, as a former detective, to help catch, the individuals at large. And may not, mention what he is up too, like most, undercover operation is handle. Never, to bring attention, to himself, as always in, the background observing criminals and their ruff nature of living. So as a former detective, Benjamin, has taking each family members past incidents, to heart, with this estrange young lady past. He needs, some kind of, lead, to get her off of, the streets quick and soon. Benjamin, will find a way. Now that the snowing has stop, Cain is trying, to go and see Sheila again. But he may be very disappointed, because, she, isn't home. But he wants, to leave, both Terra and Dana, by themselves, because, they are sitting ducks in, that so called dungeon, in which it their tomb, when Nuel send, his hitman over to lay all, to rest of course. See Cain's thoughts are, to dump, both women and move on. But he knows, Terra would try, to hunted him down, to put a bullet in him, like she, did with Nuel. And Cain still doesn't know, that Nuel is still alive and trying, to recuperating, from his wound. But Nuel is set-to take out both women, for their devastating deeds. No one shoots Nuel, and then rob, the man. So Terra has the law to deal with and Nuel as well. After everything she will go through, Terra would wish, she wasn't born at all. The thing is, who will get her first? Nuel and company, or law enforcement. Terra and crew are starting, to look like, a female John Dillinger, on the run, which made him a public enemy number one. Everyone in the law enforcement wanted Mr. Dillinger capture or dead. John Dillinger, was way ahead, before Terra's time but it doesn't change, the facts on being a person, with low self-esteem, no morals, to know, right, from wrong, no discipline whatsoever in her life. Terra, did Terra and she had really, no one, to answer too. But herself. This is when kid's trying, to be adults, knows more, then the hand, that fed them. And now, they have it all, figured out. But in reality, kids know, Crap! Just like Terra, spoiled, and she did get her way, but she didn't have it her way. Living in a foster home, her foster parents, spoiled her, to a certain extent. Until she, tried, to kill them both, it was on a cold bitter night, as her foster parents put her in bed, for the night, they go, to bed, themselves. Terra on the other hand, goes and turned, the eyes on, the stove, which the house, would smell like gas, then she would, tried, to leave. But her foster dad, got up, to use the bathroom, when he smelt, gas, then he went, to the kitchen, and the stove was on, without the pilot lit. He caught, Terra before she could, get out of, the door. That's when, the foster parents, sent her back, to the group home. Terra was trying, to blow, the house completely off, the block, with the couple inside. Now Terra will have a record, matter where she goes, and no one wants her in, their home. One case worker, describe her as a bad seed, or a bad apple, without a care in the world. A girl without love.

A Crying Confession
Chapter VI

Dana and Terra, are sitting and playing Euchre, with each other, while Cain, thinking about Sheila, and what she, could be up too. As he has a lot on, his mind, one thing is, for sure, that is getting, the heck away, from these two women. Cain is, for sure changing his ways. After talking, to Sheila, just for a moment, it had an effect on him, now Sheila, needs, to help Cain, in turning his life around, and she can be, the one, to do that. Only if he would, keep his mind and focus on, the words, that Sheila is telling him, things he needs, to know, instead of focusing on her beautiful rear end, Cain can make it, with a bright and intelligent young woman like Sheila. But once him and Sheila, make that connection, Cain will, see the very different in, the women's, he was accustomed too.

But first, he needs, to think of, a plan, to set himself free, from the aggravation under a woman leadership, that doesn't know, any right, from wrong, to save her soul. Also Cain knows, that change is required, to move on, or just keep on doing, what's best, for Terra's sake. As sitting playing a game still, there's a loud knock, at the huge steel doors. As both women, pulled their pistols, with Cain, trying, to see who it is, but can't recognized, the two huge men, at the doors. So everyone sat still and quiet, then the men, was pounding, to get some attention. These guys, are Nuel's henchmen's, to do his dirty work. Because, if Cain, would've answer, the door, they would've blasted him instead of, the women. So Cain, did right, for not answering, the doors.

As both men circle, the building, to see if anyone was inside, to opened, the door. The men came, there on orders, form their boss, which is Nuel. To get both women, and bring them back, to him, for what they did. While everyone sat still inside, but the guys, sat in their vehicle outside, the abandon building, to see what will happen. Now Cain knows, that trouble is sitting and waiting on, them outside. So Cain and the women needs, to come up, with a plan, to escape, the vengeance of Nuel's men. Both Nuel's men, are walking, with automatic Uzi's. And Cain knows, he isn't a match, for those huge men with automatic weapons. So Cain use common sense, not to opposed, these ruthless killers. But on, the other hand, it's two of them, with three of them inside. But if Terra, would get mad enough. She could, use her evilness, against both men. And Terra thought, of a plan, while the guys, was still sitting outside of, the building. Her and Dana, would be a distraction to lured, both men in, the building, kill them. But just thought of let them be. But Terra and Dana did it their way, as women to get a man, to fall into temptation as usual, and it works for them every time. Now both men are still, sitting in their vehicle, watching, the building, as Dana uses her body, to get the men, to come inside, the building. Once inside, Terra is, in a room off, to herself, for one guy, to see her, while Dana would keep, the other man at bay. With a little of intelligence and working together, equals getting, the job done. And both men are falling, for the women's plan, to seduce and kill. So Nuel's henchmen has a weakness also. Women!

The sin nature, is spilling over the place, while Cain is in hiding, for the women, to work their plan out. Because, Cain would jeopardize, their plan, if he is seen. As Dana sat the one down, to talk him out of his coat, for her to sit on, his lap, to get lovey dubby, with him, and he takes off his coat, while the other man, goes, to the room, where Terra is. When the man walks in, he was captivated, with the looks of Terra's well-being. But not knowing, the danger, that lays and wait, for him. Terra had made a pallet on, the floor, to lay on, to do her business, and then move it, when she is done. As she, was down on, her pallet, with her legs open and half way naked, for to reveal herself, to her bait, for pleasure.

And as the pigeons, walks, to the feline's, to be devoured by evil and wicked. The man, with Terra, is getting ready, to meet his maker, as climbing on top of, Terra, for pleasure. Terra puts one in his head, as Dana also puts a bullet in the chest of, the other man. Now these women, has sat, the tone, for not to go up against, anywhere, anytime and anyplace. As the women's plan works, Cain was a little impressed, how things play out, to the finished. He gave both, Terra and Dana, some credit, in not knowing, that, the women can cause, a man, to fall flat on his face, with her own tool, that is her body. A soft, warm, fragile, harmless tool, that every man wants, to cuddle with. But some tools, aren't good, to have and not to be tamper with. But with a caution, sign on it. Man still has a tendency, to go and mess with her, for his own demised.

Cain knows, that the men, were here, to kill, Dana and Terra, for shooting Nuel. But the women had turned, the situation completely around, to stay alive. But there will, be another attack, from Nuel, for Nuel's sake. Until both women are lying on, his door steps dead. Cain is getting, some assistance, from both women, to help dispose of, the huge men's bodies. "I feel really good, about, the way we handle, those men." said, Dana. As Dana, looks at Terra's eyes, to see that somethings were bothering Terra deeply. Because, lately Terra, has distance herself at times, for whatsoever reason, but Terra, can be a harsh person and a little cruel and shrewd at times also.

"Hey you, Tee, would you, like to talk about, what's eating you?" asked, Dana. "Maybe later, I think, I'm just tired, that's all." said, Terra. "I need, to make a new pallet, also, that one has that guy's brain's all over it." said, Terra. "Ladies! I'll be back, let me take, these heavy dead muth*&#^! And dump them somewhere." said, Cain. But Cain, is thinking, that this, is his time, to go and see Sheila, without any disturbance's, whatsoever. In his mind, he is the man, that is going, to meet a good woman, to be around. But it will be a distraction, because, her father, brother and uncle, will be watching from a distance, to make sure nothing happens, to her. But if so, all three men, is coming for Cain, in a way, that he could, far imagine. But before, he could go and see Sheila, he needs, to air, the van out, because, it has a stench, like no body business. Just if Sheila, might want, to get in, and talk, it would be a problem. She would have to smell, the stench, from dead men.

Cain dumped, both bodies near Murray Park, not far, from the Bentford's home. He put them there, so someone can call, the authorities or a park ranger, would discover them. But if Nuel, would know, that this is happening, Cain would be a dead man also. Therefore, Nuel, is still in, the hospital getting some rehab doing, to his body. But once he finds out, that two of his henchmen's are decease. Nuel is really, wants both women's heads. Now there is conflict, between a local gangster, and women of evil. Terra wants, the Bentford's, Nuel, wants Terra and Dana, and the authorities wants, Terra, and crew.

Now if there's a chance, to get someone, everyone has, to begotten someone else. That's not good, at all. Because, of someone else, conflict can spread, to another person, that hasn't anything, to do with, what's going on. But they found, themselves getting involved, more less dragged into it. As Cain, pulls, the last big guy out of the van, to dump him, he stood, there looking in, the direction of, the mountains, thinking how beautiful it looks, from where he stands. BUT if he goes back to a cell, those mountains, would only sit in back of his mind and never see a beautiful site again. Cain is about, to fight with his demons, within him. He wants, to turned himself in to the authorities, to get off easy, and stop running, from them and hoping, that the judge, would be very lenient with him, so he can spend time, with Sheila, if so. Because, the more he runs, the more time he may spend behind, the bars. As tears, flow down his cold cheeks, thinking of never seeing Sheila again, Cain would hurt inside bad, for not able, to see this woman.

As Cain wipes his face, from crying his guilt, to go and to see Sheila. Before it gets any later. With it getting colder out Cain is hoping, that Sheila is home. Cain's thought, if he could just see, the sight of, her. He would be alright; his evening would have turned out great. As getting back into, the van, to head over, to Sheila home, to see her. It crossed, his mind, to turned, himself into, the law. It's also, very heavy on, his heart, to do, the right thing, by talking, to Sheila, about his problems also. But being, the man he is, Cain rather, gain Sheila's friendship first, then, to make his life right first, then get, the woman last. So doing it, the way he knows, how is wrong. Cain sitting mad behind bars, when he, found out, that Sheila, has move on, with her life, with someone else. Now that's Cain's thought. As the Bentford's family returned home, for the evening, to get Benjamin all settled in, from his trip. Ben is very happy and proud, to be with his family, that he missed, so much. "I can say, now home sweet home." said, Benjamin. "Indeed, this is home, for you now Uncle Ben." said, Jon. "Oh my. What in the hell, happened, to the house?" asked Ben. As all three Sam, Jon and Sheila, looks at each other, then looks at Ben, to tell what had, transpired in, the previous months. "Ed, did, this, remember, when I told, you about a creature, that tried, to kill us, it was Ed, he was part beast, part man." said, Sam. "That muth*#$@!^! I would've had killed, his ass." said, Benjamin. "Well how much, damage did, this Asshole cost you Sammy?" asked, Benjamin. "I say ruffly, somewhere about $40,000.00." said, Sam. "Ok, we going, to make everything new, how about that?" asked, Ben.

"Well my insurance only covers, so much, and I had, to pay, for June's memorial service, then that left us not much, but something in, the account." said, Sam. "Sammy, don't worried, about it, it needs, to be done, and it shall be done." said, Ben. While everyone was standing in, the living room talking, there's a strange knock, at the door. "Who is it!?" asked, Jon. "Cain! Is Sheila here, and may I talk, to her!?" asked, Cain. Jon opened, the door, to see who was on, the other side, to see who was asking, for his sister. Sheila came, to the door, and she smiled, from ear to ear, as her eyes lit up, the porch. "Hi Cain." said, Sheila. "Hello Sheila, I'm sorry, to barge in on you and your family, I just wanted, to see you, and how you we're doing." said, Cain. "I want you, to meet my family, so come on in." said, Sheila. "Well ok." said, Cain. "Hey everyone, this is Cain, is a friend, that I met on, the front porch, his van stop on him, out here in, the front." said, Sheila. "This is my father Sam, that's my brother Jon, and that's my uncle Benjamin." said Sheila. "Again, hello, to you all." said, Cain. "Well Sheila, I'm not, staying long, I need, to be getting home. "said, Cain. "Well Cain, I'm, so glad, to see you again, next time you come over, and stay for dinner, how about that?" asked, Sheila. "I would love, that absolutely." said, Cain. "Well how about, this weekend coming?" asked, Sheila. "Great, say no more, my dear lady, I'll be here." said, Cain. "Alright, dear man, have yourselves, a good evening." said, Sheila. Cain walking, to the van humming a song, he hasn't heard, in years. But he is feeling so good about himself, that he forgot all about his personal calamity, with life. With him on a cloud isn't going, to hold him very long. Because, soon enough, the law is coming for him and the women, soon enough, for the disappearance of a sheriff deputy, who's cruiser was found in, the back yard, of Ed's old house. Sheriff Protzman's, suspected, that Terra and her followers, had something, to do with him gone. Now the law enforcement is very heavy, for fugitives, that's on the run, and murder, a deputy as well. So Sheriff Protzman's team is taking every avenue it gets, to catch, these young criminals, before lots of people die, for no reason. Now the year is 1981 and Sheriff Protzman's technology is getting an upgrade with a better way, to serve, the public with accuracy and efficiency, when dealing with crime. The Deputy, that is missing is a 16-year veteran name Donald Fluk who was promoted to sergeant. He had one year, to go before making lieutenant, and now, no one knows, where he is, but the department had found his cruiser in, the back yard of Ed Dart's old abandon house. Between Cain, Dana or Terra no one is keep tabs on the evening news, that has their mugshots on all across, the television. It's so sad, that Cain, isn't aware of this. While he's trying, to be with Sheila. As embarrassment, knocking on his door, to come in, and turned, his world upside down, For him, to be humiliated and frustrated, to where he would give up, then death would finish things up in a unique way. But it would make him run again, from his problems. This is where a young guy, doing things his way, because, in his heart, he is right matter what. If he finds out, that his mugshot and the woman's mugshot is exposed, this would cause, them, to run even more, from the authorities. It's really, crazy, to have gangster's and law enforcement's, to be after you at, the same time, So Cain, has come, to his senses, by getting arrested, to save himself, from being a homicide victim. The Sheriff department, found DNA, that belongs, to Cain Gordillo, Cain hit the officer in the head, with a pipe, then he dropped it, and left it near, the back porch. So now, a manhunt is on, for him, for sure.

On his way back, to the women, Cain stop, for a sandwich and a beer, at the diner. Soon as he walks in, he notices, that a crowd of people, was staring at him. But Miguel, pulled him aside, to tell him the bad news, that his mugshots and his women associates are on the t.v. "And the law is, looking for you all." said, Miguel. Miguel let Cain, use his back door, to the diner, to escape, the crowed, that's in front of, the diner. As he avoided, the crowd, to get out of, site before someone can point him out. Running to his van, to making it back, to the hideout, to let the others know, that serious trouble is headed their way.

As slowing down, at the traffic light, Cain notice, a deputy's cruiser, sitting off, to his left on, an empty lot. But lucky he, no one wasn't in it. So as he, was driving, he thought of, going by Sheila house, to explained, his situation, to her plain and clearly, that it made shed some light on his t.v appearance. His thoughts, on keep on running, from everything, including her also. Now Cain, wishing he, could've told, her then and there while on her porch, but not thinking properly. Then thoughts, of her seeing, him already making him sick, to his stomach. So he goes, to see her again, with it being late in the evening, to get, this monkey off of, his back. Cain arrived, by pulling, the van across, from the house next, to the corn field. Getting out, with a nervous feeling, hoping, that Sheila didn't see, the news at all. Knocking on, the door, Jon answers, the door, to see who it was, he notices, that it was Cain, Jon, calls Sheila, to the door, while Cain was out on, the porch, in a nervous wreck, to speak, to Sheila. Sheila, came, to the door, with all smiles as usual, to see a guy, she starts, to show a bit of, interested in. "Hey, again, are you, ok?" asked, Sheila. "Sheila, I have, some explaining, to do, I know, I haven't been real, with you. But I falling, in love, with you, the day I met you, and now it's getting ready, to fall apart, for me." said, Cain. "Why apart?" asked, Sheila.

"Sorry, haven't you, seen, the news?" asked, Cain. With Sheila's eyes widing opening, her whole demeanor, changed with an instant. "What are you, talking about sweetie?" asked, Sheila. "I'm a fugitive on, the run, from the law." said, Cain. "And please, don't push me away." said, Cain. "You need, to leave. You need, to leave, right now!" said, Sheila. "Sheila." said, Cain. As Sheila, goes inside, without saying good bye, or good night. It made Cain think, that there's no friendship, not ever again. But only in his mind. But his heart, will always before her, rather she knows, it or not. Cain's thoughts, that Sheila, will be his in, the coming months. As he let, the justice's system, do what it's gonna do. As Sheila, come in, to the house, goes straight, to her room, and not say a word, about Cain's situation, she doesn't want her father, uncle and big brother, to know, anything of, the situation, that she is now aware of. But what really, struck Sheila, in the whole soft conversation, was that, Cain said, that he, fell in love, with her. And that, has her mind and heart wanting him as well. Sheila's thoughts, of having another man in her life, could take her mind off of, Jay, that being gone, for a year and a half.

But she, never, thought of having a thug, gangster and fugitive on, the run kinda guy like Cain. Who shows, the enthusiasm, that he, really care, for, this woman's wellbeing. Cain did, right by confessing his run, from the law, but couldn't finished, the rest, before Sheila leaving him alone. Now that Cain is driving back, to the hideout, he cried, for a moment, the hurt, will linger, for a season, but a soft face, with a warm smile, will always last forever in minds and hearts. But before, returning, to the hideout, Cain went, to his, main place of peace, that is under a bridge, that is called, Optimistic Crossing, where he would, go to clear his head, before facing his trouble's. Then think on doing, the right thing. As it getting colder, he was trying, to find a place, to sit, from the wind.

While sitting still, wasn't helping him, to keep warm, but thinking of Sheila's smiles what kept, him from freezing, as he has flashbacks of her face. "That's it! I'll turned myself in." said, Cain. "If I'm, going, to be with, Sheila, I would have to make it right." said, Cain. Cain thinking out loud. Meanwhile back at, the hideout, both women are trying, to keep warm in, that big abandon building, in which is hard, to do, with a lot of space. Nothing but air, and madness of cold, with both women are shuddering and trembling. Asking one another about Cain. It's so cold, to both women, they starting talking about unnecessary things, that no one cares, to share with. Until Terra, started, talking about herself. "Dana, I haven't had a man, to impregnate me yet, I thought, that Jon, might do, the trick, but I guess not." said, Terra. "Dana, is something, wrong, with me?" asked, Terra. "Oh Honey, I think nothing is wrong." said, Dana. "What I think, is you need a guy a good guy, to make you feel good, about being a woman." said, Dana. But Dana, I haven't had a period in months." said, Terra. As she started, to cried, to confessing of a naughty little secret, that she maybe robs of being a woman, with something growing inside of her.

As Dana stood and stared, at Terra, showing some optimistic on her part. "Tee, tell me this, why is one of your eyes, holds a different color, then the other? Why is your hair, grows by the minute, and not mention, your nails girl!?" asked, Dana. "I have a special gene, from my father, that was pass, to me." said, Terra. "What kinda, of gene!?"

asked, Dana. "Well I can't tell you, everything, because, I don't know, myself." said, Terra. "If I had your genes, I would probably be super woman." said, Dana, with a laugh. "Well it has it moment, when I'm upset and around men especially, because, men can cause my estrogens and hormones levels, to act up." said, Terra.

"Because, the way they think and act, as a man." said, Terra. "Like the Bentford's, for instant, I didn't not like neither one of them at all, but I had a job, to do by wrecking up, that family, for the sake of my father." said, Terra. "I tried, to kill both men, but the father, had gotten, the best of me, by hitting me in, the head, to knock me out cold, but also I still have a plan, for his ass." said, Terra. As both women sat together, to keep each other warm, by hold each other hands, while talking about men in general, with a bit of femininity, until Dana started, to stare, Terra in, the face, then Dana kissed Terra on, the lips. But Terra was so completely speechless, but she, like it at, the same time. Then Dana holds, Terra in her arms, "So I think, that this is what I was looking, for you and I to have a moment, to find, that right spot and time." said, Terra. "So this, makes us girlfriends now, I take it?" asked, Terra.

"I always needed you, the day I laid eyes on you." said, Dana. "We don't need a man, but only his money and help, with the heavy stuff." said, Dana. Before Dana, could tell, Terra, that she loves her, a loud noise outside, the place. "What in, the world, was that?" asked, Terra. As both women, goes and take a look, to see what seem, to be the problem. "Shh, there are four guys, with guns out here in front of, this place, and where is Cain, he is being out of actions, for a while." said, Dana.

"So what are we going, to do?" asked, Dana. The four guys are sent by Nuel, to find, the other two guys he sent before, in which they are presumably dead. They were sent, to kill, the two women, but never came back, to give a report or nothing. So Nuel's crew, sent another hit team, to do the job, and make sure, they come with a report of, the two women are decease. Now as both women are thinking of, doing what they did before, with the last two guys, but this is different, with four and could be very dangerous. They could kill, the two and the other two could cover the other two. So the women, kept quiet and very still, until the men left. So Terra thinks, that Nuel is still alive, with a set of guys with weapons, keep coming here, to get them. "Why is it, that we keep seeing, these guys pop up, with weapon, trying, to get in here?" asked, Terra.

Again, the women pulled it off, they know, that a four men crew, to take on two women, was a little bit extreme, for both women, to handle. But Nuel, won't stop until he gets what he wants. His men, will keep on coming, until the ladies are dead, then they will stop. But the women must be put in their proper resting place, then Nuel, would have what he wanted. The Reyes crime family isn't, to be mess with. Nuel only has a day, to get back, to his life, as a Latin gangster. Getting rid of, these two women, may come, with a price, that the gangster, isn't aware of. But he not going away, until someone is dead. See Nuel, isn't mad about, the money, they took, it's the pride of a gangster, they distraught. Especially when Terra shot him, for no apparent reason. So that hurts him bad, until now he wants, the women's head, served, to him on a platter. And with, all that, just agitated, the hell out of him. Being in, the hospital, to get well. But only a day, to go, then it's hunting season, for the mobster on two worthless chicks'. But Nuel, doesn't know, that the law enforcement is also looking for these two women and Cain as well. But that wouldn't stop Nuel, from putting a contract on both women heads. The way it looks, like an all-out war on two women and a man. But Terra has another plan, to take on, Nuel's henchmen's, with her power, from this parasite. But Dana, wouldn't be in no kinda danger, by working next, to Terra's creature. Terra has matured enough, to handle, the transformation, from woman, to she-creature. Her invisible power, will take place only, when she is threatened by danger.

So now is the time, as good as ever, to exercise, her powers of destruction, to be like her father's ways of doing things. Absolutely killing is in her blood, and now she can move like her father. Terra eats, sleep, and breathe killing, this is her blood linage, to set out, to destroyed whomever and whenever. Now as the women, get strangely bold, to go and destroyed, the house, that Nuel, has built, to get a handle on, the men, who is trying, to kill them. It may be rough and tough, to go up against thirty plus men. But a two on thirty, can be extremely, too much, to come out clean, from a bullet. In other words, the women aren't concerned, about the odds, they are going, to destroyed, the odds and leave, the place, for a message, from a deadly destruction of evil was here. As both women, gather up as much ammunition, for their weapons, but Dana is the one with, the weapons, while Terra is in a form of a creature, so she, isn't going, to need a weapon, because, she is a weapon, a force herself, to be reckon with. Therefore, both ladies have arrived, near Nuel's compound, to make, the place a peaceful cemetery of men. Every man, that is there, will have a taste of death. Dana needed, a diversion, to draw as many men her way, for Terra, to make her way inside, to put as many men, to sleep by death. With some of, the men, just standing guarding, the other side of, the compound, isn't aware of the attack is going on. Until Dana, made a loud explosion, by shooting a transformer, to kill the power, for the men to bump into each other, with leaving everyone confused, about what is happening.

As both women making noise all through, the compound, inside and out. With blood splatter everywhere, and guns going off, with Dana, having, the gift, to see most anything in the dark, and not miss her target. Terra, is doing what she knows, best, and that is, to kill. She, is going, though, this compound and lying men in, their own blood, until the place is full of dead men, with red walls. Like Terra, was painting, the walls red, that evening. The place was full of screams and shooting, as Terra goes up the stairs, to find, anything, that is still breathing, to destroy him, and move on. As Dana, taking care, of those that was outside, she makes her way inside, to help her girlfriend and protégé, to finished up destroying this house.

The women made, Nuel's compound, into a tomb of men, and Nuel isn't aware, that his home is a tomb, with dead men all over, the place inside and out. What a surprise, to come into a domain, with a stench, from death. Now that the women came, to do, to what needed, to be done, Dana yells, for Terra. But Terra didn't answer yet. Because, she, was invisible and standing next, to Dana. But scared Dana, until she fired, her weapon. While Terra needs, to transformed back, to herself she goes, to a place, inside, this compound, to go back, to her usual self. As her and Dana, just standing there looking at all that they had created, so on Nuel's returned, he, will not be very please, at the site of things. And not knowing, he has lost over at less, a hundred men, under his leadership.

And many more, if he's, contemplating in pursuiting, them again. He might as well, gone and give up, for chasing a woman, that knows, how, to kill without thinking. If Nuel's release, later on, today, he is welcome home, to a slaughter tomb of men, that was on his payroll, to protected his mansion and other assess. But Nuel is by all means, of not backing down for nobody and from no one at all. All this man, is going, to do is, hire more men power, to get hold of, the situation quickly and resolved it with a bullet. Now there is one problem, that will disturb him, so completely. That is his surveillance system will show, him what went down, with all his men. That Terra and Dana is expose, and Nuel may see, that Terra had changed, into a creature like. There are cameras all over, the place, even over, the pool. So whatever went down, the monitors, will not lie, but the evident, lays in front. There's no doubt about it, Nuel did hired, the best men, that his money can buy, but a couple of women proved him wrong, by coming in and taking all by surprise. Lot of his men have killed recently and in the past also.

With all that is going on with Nuel and these women. Their minds have left, the Bentford's to rest, from engaging a fight with them as well. But Nuel, takes this vendetta personally, to a new level, until now it's getting really ugly between, the women and a gangster and his outfit. As Nuel, on his way home from the hospital, he tried, to reach one of his men and the phone kept ringing. "What the f#@$! where is everybody?!" asked Nuel. Now he calls up his cousin, to pick him up, and take him home. "Hey Miguel, can you come, and take me home?" asked, Nuel. "I be there, after I make sure, my diner, is secured." said, Miguel. "Give me twenty minutes." said, Miguel.

As sitting in the lobby, Nuel, was thinking what in the hell is going on in my house? Nuel thought. Meanwhile the women had made it back, to the hideout, to remove everything out as they thought, Because, if Nuel is still alive, that means he is coming in full force, for a bigger fight, for the slaughter of his men. "What about the Bentford's? Are we going, to get them too?" asked, Dana. "No we will be next, to them in my dad's old shack, and then we will go and get them as well." said, Terra. But right now, we have to get out of here." said, Terra. When both women had pulled, in front of the building, they can see, that the van is back, so that means, "Cain is inside, to help us move, then we kill him as well. Because, he's not reliable anymore, to us, So Dana, get rid of him." said, Terra. As both women approached Cain, to help with all the personal stuff, to load, the van up, to get out of here. "Hey we are on the t.v everywhere!" said, Cain. As the women looked with a bewilder confuse face, knowing, that trouble is really closing in on them in a hurried. So with the Gangster and law enforcement on, their tails, and trying to engage havoc with the Bentford's would be an all-out war, for a mess, they started and can't finished, for one it would be a one-sided war and a catastrophe, for both women. Because, the law will prevail against them. No matter where, they go, the law is still in a hot pursuit, catch them one way or another. As all three, put stuff onto, the van, to run to the shack, that's in, the middle of nowhere, to hide for a while. But if they are looking, for things, to blow over, they're out of their minds. "Well ladies! I'm going, my own way now, beside we ought to split up, anyway I must head south, to escape, this madness." said, Cain. "You are a no-good bastard!! you know, that you unreliable missing in action f@#$!" said,

Dana. "what in, the hell is your problem?" asked, Cain. "Terra! You better, put your girl in check!" said, Cain. "No! Cain! Why don't we put you in check! how about that?" asked, Terra. "Look! We need, to go, before someone see us." said, Cain. Cain has a semi auto in his back, so if things get hot, with him and the women, he said, before get the drop on Dana first, then Terra. Because, Cain knows, that things aren't sweet like it used to be, as things turns sour in, the crew, Cain is making a move, to turn himself into, the law. Because, running isn't getting him nowhere, but in trouble. Therefore, as planned, the women is still wants, to do Cain in. But Cain knows, that these two are up, to nothing good. "I believe they are going together."

Cain thought. As the evening, has fall, it's getting colder by the minutes, with moving, from a cold place, to another, isn't setting well, with the women. And Terra and Dana, both needs, a hot shower, to get those men stench off. As everything is loaded and ready, to go, Terra and Dana, jumps on Cain, for one last time, to get rid of him also. "So Cain! where was you, when we really needed you, when these mutha*&%$# keep showing up with guns, trying, to get in here, to do us in?" asked, Terra. "Well if you must know, I was somewhere minding my owned, F***ing business! trying, to lay low and stay off of the radar!" said, Cain. "Like I said, we are on, the evening news, if that means anything, to you at all." said, Cain. "Well C.G. Are you with us, or not!?" asked, Terra. "No! I'm going, on my own, and I my just turn myself into the law." said, Cain.

The minute, Cain has said, what he said, the both Terra and Dana, pulled, their weapons, and Cain, pulled his also and pointed it at Dana head. So now it's a standoff a guy and two gals, trying to scare each other. "So C.G. I take it, that you going to rat us out, to the f***ing authorities?" asked, Dana. "Far as I can see it, who cares, what you women think, I'm so tired of running, from the law it's making me miserable with others, I haven't had a woman in a while, So I'm trying to do right with my life." said, Cain. As both women surrounding him, as he talks sense, into them as well. "Hey you do you, we do we!" said, Terra. "Ok! Let's do that then." said, Cain. "Ok we are out of here, with you or without you." said, Terra. Cain went, to the van, to pulled his personal belongings out of the van, before Terra and Dana, decides, to take off. Without saying goodbye, to each other. But Cain was cool with that, as long it wasn't any shooting among them. So Cain will turn himself into the authorities as he prepared, to do one more visit, to see Sheila, for the last time. Then he will let the authorities know, where to pick him up.

Across town, Nuel returned, to his residences, with things not looking right, in front of his home. Miguel and Nuel, was confused at looking at men lying in front of his place, they both didn't know what, to do. Soon as both men walk into, the foyer, they smell an awful stench, that would make a hog regurgitate. "What the f***! happened here?!" asked, Miguel. "Cousin! Are you in trouble?" asked, Miguel. Nuel, just ignored, his cousin's remarks, while he was trying his best, to figured out what had happened. So he made his way, to his audio closet, to look at what, the cameras had pick up. "Well look who we have here!" said, Nuel. "Those b**ches, came back!! to destroyed all my men!" said, Nuel. "Wait a minute cousin! that's the women, that the law enforcement are looking for, so you had these women in your house?!" asked, Miguel. "Cousin, these are some bad women, you shouldn't mess with them." said, Miguel. "Miguel!! who in the f*** I'm I, or you forgot, that I run, this side of the town, far as those b**ches! I will have their heads, before the law can catch up to them. Now that Nuel know, who attacked his home and declared war on his men, this has stirred, the pot, for the war, to go as longer. "This is so pitiful!! to see thirty men dead by two women!!!" said, Nuel. "This isn't fair, at all." said, Nuel. "Hey Cousin! call Fargas, for help, him and his men could give us a hand, and you know, he has some of the best killers around." said, Miguel. "I hate, to bother him, and besides, I don't want to see him, and his men, in body bags or wearing toe tags, so I might, just leave him out of this, and this is between them and I." said, Nuel. "Like my men, all in body bags, with all wearing that toe tag. Of course!" said, Nuel. "The war, is far, from being over, you can bet on that! Who these, b**ches, think they are?!" asked, Nuel. "Nuel! Do you know, where to find them?" asked, Miguel. "Of course! their asses are at, the old abandon water treatment facility, that's where I took a stolen car, to Cain, so they should be there." said, Nuel. "Well what are we waiting for?" asked, Miguel. It was very frustrated, for Nuel, to see all his men deceased, for whatever purpose it proves, but he isn't done rolling, the dice of death, to have someone else's life, to crap out. Nuel is the biggest kingpin in the west, that the mountains have produce. As Nuel calls on, a private crew, to come into do some cleaning by putting all of, the dead corpse in body bag, and clean, the blood off of the walls, and he urged, them, to remove, the corpse, from around, the pool, because, of his nosey neighbors. But his neighbors know, not to mess, with him or even look, his way. So Nuel, with his cousin, Miguel, has come up with a brilliant ideal, to do harm, without notice, to the authorities. As the O.G that Nuel is, he raised, the contract, to a million dollars dead or alive, for both women. The women don't know, if Nuel is still alive, far as they know, Nuel is dead. If Terra, would've put a bullet in the head of Nuel, they wouldn't be in, this mess. Now Nuel is watching all his men, be hauled off, to the morgue in body bags. It was a day of reckoning, for his men. Wishing that he never, met Terra or showing them, where he lives. But one thing is, for sure, that is a death for a death. As it plays in his head, the evening when he got shot in, the shoulder, if he could only know, their plans, to kill him, it would've saved his men, from being slaughter. So as Nuel, thinking about what could've, and should've not, left a hard lump in his throat.

"After the cleanup, crew leave, we will also." said, Nuel. "Ok" said, Miguel. While walking up his stairwell, to his bedroom, Nuel noticed an unusual scent, that he never ever, came across in his mansion, so he went, to room to room, to see what is that horrible stench, but couldn't find it. "Hey Miguel! Do you smell that!?" asked, Nuel. "Hey Nuel! It your top lip! Hahaha!" said, Miguel, with a sense of humor. But Nuel, just looked at him, without a smile, with a face of madness. But when

Nuel walked into, his hall bathroom, there was the scent of, a creature like salivate on the floor, that smells so horrible, that it makes a billy goat regurgitate. It was making Nuel sick, by just smelling it. Miguel had to drag his cousin outside for air. Miguel went back inside, to have, one of the guys, to clean up, that which is in, the floor of, the bathroom.

While Nuel, was sitting next, to his pool, he thought of going to shoot Cain also, for not giving him, the heads up, about his girl's being ruthless as can be. But he not going, to do that, cause, Cain did, warned him of her. (Terra). Cain is trying, to get up enough courage, to go and see Sheila, before turning himself into the hands of the authority. But he's not telling, where Terra and Dana are at, just him along. Cain is only the one inside of, the abandon facility, but getting ready, to go see Sheila. But before, he could get into, the car. Two guys pulled up and block him, from leaving. Cain goes over, to see what the hell, this is all about. And it's Nuel, and Miguel. And Cain looked very surprising, to see a dead Nuel, in good formed. "Hey fellows! what's up!?" asked, Cain. "You is up, you is a piece, of s**t, Cain!" said, Nuel. "Where are, those b**ches at!?" asked, Nuel. "Hey they left me, here by myself, they took off without me!" said, Cain. "You know, where?" asked, Nuel. "Nope. I don't know anything." said, Cain.

"You know, what I think is, that you know, and you're not trying, to tell me anything!" said, Nuel. As Nuel and Miguel both get out and surround Cain, to bully him, for information about the women's whereabouts. "I just want, to talk, to them." said, Nuel. "Well you don't mind, if we take a look, for ourselves do you?" asked, Nuel. As walking through, the empty building, they found nothing, but pipes and a stench of a smell. "I told, you, they aren't here anymore." said, Cain. "I had to check, for myself, it's that I don't believe you, it's the deceit I don't trust." said Nuel. "Oh by the way, how's the car running?" asked, Nuel. "Ok I guess." said, Cain. "Well this might, be my last time, me seeing you." said, Cain. "Why is that, I may ask?" asking,

Nuel. As Cain pause. "I'm turning myself into the authority, I'm tired, of running, from the law enforcement, dodging, looking over my shoulders, everywhere I look, so the best thing, I can do is, the right thing." said, Cain. As Miguel and Nuel, had a bewilder look on their faces, they were speechless, at Cain's saying. They didn't know, exactly how, to cope, with that, he just said. "So Cain, are you, going, to rat on us, because, I can take, care of that right about now, if I need too?" Nuel, asked. "I didn't see you at all." said, Cain. "Well good man, and good luck, at whatever you decide, to do." said, Nuel. "Miguel, let's go!" said, Nuel.

As the men part ways, Cain went in the opposite direction, but he noticed, that both men turned, to following him, to see if he's, is tell, the truth about, the women's whereabouts. Cain knows, where the women are staying, and will not give Nuel the information, So Nuel had Miguel, to followed Cain, to see where exactly is he going. But soon or later, Cain is intelligent, with street smarts and a cold-hearted killer. In which he is trying, to put his past behind him, once and for all. Cain is taking, the men over Sheila's place. That is a bad ideal, to have, the men to followed him there. So what does, Cain do he takes, the men on a little goose chase, into the next two counties, until they decide, to stop following him.

They know, that he also knows, their game also well, so he played their game too. They thought, that he would lead them to the women, where they thought wrong, if Cain is going, to lead them to his former friends almost enemies, they would be sadly mistaken. Cain is really changing, the way he is doing things, he could've had given, those women up, for to be murder, but didn't, because, his heart is seeing things into a different perspective, instead of going left, he is choosing, to go right, to be with a woman, that means so much, to him. If that's what it will take, he is, ready to die, for her as well. As Cain, getting ready, to run out of gas, he pulls into, the nearest gas station, wandering, how is he about, to get gas, without any money on him, so an elderly lady pulls into the handicap pump, to wait for someone, to come and service her car, but no one saw her, because, the place is extremely swamp with business. So Cain, does the unthinkable, by servicing the lady. Cain did her windows and fill her car up, and checked her additives, to see how low she is, then he asked, for the total of thirty dollars, for the gas, and she gave him a fifty, for twenty-dollar tip. But Cain, did something wrong, he went into, the station, to pay for his gas of twenty dollars. "Get me twenty on pump #7." said, Cain. But his conscience, was ringing into his ears, and he is, ignoring his conscience, by holding onto, the elderly lady gas money, so it makes, that the lady stole her gas and not paid, for it. So Cain isn't clean enough, to handle his reality just as yet. He still has ways to go. While he was paying, the clerk, for the gas, Cain looks up, on the t.v, and there was a mugshot of him and both of the women. Cain walks, quickly, to the car, to get out of there in a hurry, before he could be spotted by someone. Cain drives off, like a mad man on booze, as he heads, to see Sheila, before it gets any later. But whoa! There's Nuel and Miguel, far back, it's looks like they aren't giving up, from following Cain again. While both cars are speeding, there is a speed trap up ahead, but Cain slows down enough, within a decent speed limit, but Nuel and Miguel, didn't, so here come the deputy, to pulls them over. While Cain going about his way, looking in his rear-view mirror laughing at what's behind him. "That was close." Cain, thought. Now Nuel and Miguel, sitting and arguing with each other in front of the deputy, until he told, them both, to quiet down. Then the deputy, went back, to his cruiser to run, their plates and Miguel license. But nothing was found, so he let, them go on a warning. Now loosing Cain, is like looking, for a needle in a hay stack, but not easy, to find him, as he is still a fugitive on, the run. Now Cain has arrived in front of Sheila's home, to say goodbye, for the last time, before, he heads down, to the Sheriff's office, to turned himself in.

Cain is so nervous, to see the woman, he has thought of, for a while. And now he come face to face, for one last time, with a kiss in mind. He knocks, on the door, but he hears, a lot of talk on the other side of the door, Jon comes to see who it is, he looks out, to see that it is Cain, but was very hesitant in opening, the door, because, Jon seen Cain's mugshot on the wall, at the store. So he called, Sheila, before opening, the door. "Sheila! Cain is, out here on the porch!" said, Jon. Sheila was in, the back, putting on something, that is warm, to go out, to hold a conversation, with Cain. And she did, tried, to look good, for him, to say, the three words, that a woman, likes, to hear. (You look good). As Sheila grabs her dads' jacket, to put on, to step out, to talk, with Cain. Sheila came, to the door, looking gorgeous, for Cain's eyes only, to say the words Sheila opening the door, to go out, to talk, to Cain, And she, was very delighted, in seeing Cain. But did acknowledge her beauty right off, the back. "Wow, Sheila, you look great to me." said, Cain. "Cain, thank you." said, Sheila. "Well I come, to say goodbye and I need, to do the right thing in turning myself in, but before, I do that, I needed, to see you again, before all ends well." said, Cain. "That's great, to hear Cain." said, Sheila. But let's not, say goodbye, to each other, because, I'm planning on, see you again." said, Sheila. As the words hit Cain, like a tone of love, with a grip on his heart. With that said, Cain grab Sheila, and kiss her unexpectedly, but Sheila wanted him, to do that, then she grabs him and she did the same. "Sheila, would, you be my girlfriend?" asked, Cain. As Sheila stared, into Cain's blue eyes, with a smile and glow in her greyish eyes. "I love to be with you, but you must get through, your situation first ok?" asked, Sheila.

"Ok, of course, I fell in love, with you months ago, and I said, to myself, that I want her, for my lovely lady." said, Cain. "I didn't know, you months ago, so where did you see me at besides here?" Sheila, asked. "Well I'm talking, about here, I'm sorry Sheila." said, Cain. "You better not, be hiding any secrets buddy, it could cost you your relationship." Sheila, said. "So tell me, whatever did, you do, for to go back to jail?" Sheila, asked. "I'm not proud, to say it, but a guy asks me, to buy him beer, and when I refused, he decide to spit on me. So I took a pipe like object, and beat him with, and I killed him." said, Cain. "Oh sweetie, no you didn't." Sheila, said.

The Wrong Man
Chapter VII

"In reality, I'm a teddy bear, not a bad person, not at all, but if someone spit on me, now it's time, to fight." Cain, said. "I know, where you are coming from, believe me." Sheila, said. "So you are trying, to be a change man, by giving up your old ways, I take it?" Sheila, asked. "Yes, ma'am indeed." said, Cain. "it's cold out here! Let talk, in my car, shall we?" Cain, asked. "Ok, let me let my family know, where I'm." Sheila, said. As both Cain and Sheila, walking, to the car, the brother and uncle, are keeping a close eye on Sheila, being with Cain. But Jon hasn't exposed Cain, to his uncle and father as of yet. In which, will drive Sam nuts. Because, when it comes, to Sheila, Sam would hurt someone, for messing, with his baby girl. Sam doesn't want anyone, to mess with either of his children. Meanwhile and not, too far off, from the Bentford's, their enemies, are over the way, plotting, to strike, at a vulnerable time, when lest unexpected. Terra still, has her sight on getting Sam for her hostage and Sheila her play toy. But on one thing Terra and Dana doesn't know, that Cain is involved with the enemy's daughter. But if both women, would find out about this betrayal, they would try, their best, to lured him, to kill him, for his Benedict Arnold ways. So with all, the tools, that her father (Ed) had left for her to use, Terra will use them. It's business as usual. Terra grabs her father's scope, to zoom in on, the Bentford's house, to see any activity going on. They don't know, that Cain, is in front of the house, with Sheila in his car talking about being together, after jail.

Therefore, another problem has occurred, with Nuel and Miguel, they had found Cain with Sheila, in his car. They pulled behind him, to see who's in the car with him, then the both of them get out, to talk with Cain again. "What the heck! These two guys are getting on my nerves." said, Cain. "Who are they?" Sheila, asked. "Cain! Cain, Cain, What are you doing here!?" Nuel, asked. "It looks like he is minding, his own business!" said, Sheila. "Honey! I'm not talking to you, I was talking, to Cain!" said, Nuel. "Well I was talking, to you!" said, Sheila. "Cain, put your lady in check." said, Nuel. "Sheila, it's ok." said, Cain. "Now what do you guys want!?" Cain, asked.

"We thought, you were turning, yourself into, the authorities, if I was you, I would, make a run, for the border, and want look back." Nuel, said. "Well asshole, you aren't him." Sheila, said. "C'mon hon, why do I have, to be all of that?" asked, Nuel. Sheila, just ignored him. As Nuel, walks on, the other side of the car to get to Sheila, and when he does, he grabs her by the neck, while Miguel had a knife on Cain. With a stroke of luck, Jon happens, to glance out, the window, and things, didn't look right, to him, from a distant, so he goes, to the door, to really see what's going down. "Hey!! what the f*** are you doing man!!?" said, Jon. Now Sam and Benjamin come out, to see, for themselves as well. Nuel let Sheila, go and Miguel put away his knife. "Miguel vamos!" Nuel, said. As he talks some Spanish in frustration. Leaving in a bit of anger. As he turns, to Cain, to let him know," this isn't over yet Cain!" said, Nuel. "Whatever man! For as I'm concerned, Go to hell, and don't touch, my lady again! You hear me?" Cain, asked. As Nuel and Miguel, takes off, like a couple of robbers, that just hit a bank. "Sheila! Honey, you and your friend, c'mon in, it's freakin cold out here." said, Sam. As going into the house, Cain grabs Sheila's hand and holding it tight, for whatever reason, but he made sure, that Sheila wasn't leaving nowhere. As soon as Cain, comes through, the front door, Jon pulled his glock automatic, and told, Cain, to sit down and not to move. Cain did as he was told, with all three men, had him corner, for some answers about his mugshot, and why is he running, from the law and what was all, that about in front of the house? "Hey guy! I don't know, you but whatsoever you got going on, take that s***! some other place, don't ever bring, that around here, beside you could've had, my daughter hurt, over your bullcrap! So did I make myself clear?" Sam, asked. "Yes sir! Loud and clear." Cain, said. Now Nuel and Miguel has beef, with a couple of women. And now a family, they have to content with also. Because, Nuel still haven't gotten the answer, that he is looking for. That is Terra and Dana's whereabouts. So he could kill them both, that is, what he is so utterly set to do. So he will do what's necessary, to hound Cain, with all means necessary. With getting shot, by two women who he can't get a grip on is sickening to his stomach. It kinda, reminds him, of out-of-town assassins who would come in to town, to do a job, then when the job would be completed, they get paid, to leave the town and head home. So it's not a dull moment, for a cold and bitter winter in Lajunta Colorado, with grudges and vendettas in play, the town can consider tyranny in all directions, for it to be a peaceful town. Where everyone is doing it share, to keep peace and prosperity. But a few, that is not for peace, but for every diabolical way, to seize power over a family with die hard values, and only living well, to the means of others. So with Cain, coming into, these people lives, can change who he is, or not. But it's completely up, to Cain himself, for change. With him sitting in, the midst of them, and being interrogated by uncle Benjamin, now if his seat, it's hot by now, of course it will be, after Benjamin's Q/A. Cain knows, these people are here, to help him, not to hurt him or to judge him. But love, to see what's good, for the young man, who is in love, with an older woman, like Sheila. So is Sheila, the key, to Cain wellbeing, or a cougar, with a cub, to take care of him, let's say, they take care of each other for old time's sake. But the thing is, that Sheila, needs, to get to know, Cain a little better, before a relationship, could be developed, Cain still have some tendencies about him, that isn't quite solved. He still has that, ruff nature about him, alone with his street smarts and cleverness about him. Look out! Because, a bad boy like him, you can't take the badness out of the boy, but you can, remove the boy, from, the bad. Cain could live as a decent man, if he likes, by staying out of trouble, doing the right thing, not slipping into old ways and tried, to make up for being unrighteous. Growing up can be a pain, for some young. But some growing often fast, without thinking what's ahead, for them. With 1, 2 and 3 they grown, but have, the world all figured out, and not know, which way is down, and tried up, instead of straight. Cain, never had a parent's, to love him. Cain was from foster homes, to the streets, to where, his love and nurture, came from, the streets. Only mother and father, he knew, was crime, that fed him all the avenues, he needed to know, for in order to survived. Say Sheila, had, that loving family, to look too, for comfort. With all civilized respected, from her mother June, father Sam and to her older brother, that's love. Therefore, her parents were very loving parents, to her and brother Jon. But Sam, had a great time raising his two children, it could have been three, but June had a miscarriage, with their first. But the Doctors couldn't pinpoint, the problem, with her reproduction system, so her and Sam, waited a few more years, before Jon, had showed up. Then Sheila came, to make the family complete.

By being interrogated, Cain let the three men know, that his intentions, was to see Sheila, before turning himself into, the authorities. "But I must see her, before I turned myself in, I do love your daughter, Mister B. Sheila means a lot, to me." said, Cain. As Sheila stood there, with tears of joy, hearing those precious words, was a taste of candy, to a girl's mouth. "Son that's all fine and dandy, but I think, that you and my daughter both needs, to get to know, one another first, don't you think? Sam, asked. Because, if anything happens, to her, boy, I would be hot sauce, all over your ass like a piece of chicken." Sam, said. "And that's not good, and you have to content with her brother also." said, Sam.

Therefore, is, this a rogue way, for Cain to delivered Sheila, to his boss Terra, or if he's for real, about everything he is saying? But time will tell, but he heard, every word, that Sam had enlightening him with. For his own good, like mess up boy, and prepared, to die. With what Sam, being through, in the previous year, with his wife's disappearance and death the son in law's death and Ed's ways of deceitfulness, was enough, to put Sam into a coma, but stay strong, throughout his matters and almost lost Jon, with a stabbing, from that evil b**ch of a daughter of Ed's (Terra). So endurance, from Sam with all of that. Be damn, if he's going through, that again. By losing his children again, to deceit would be very devastating, to his health. So that's why Sam is so on the defensed, side of things. It's ashamed, that a friendship, for many years, had to turned deadly, from envy, no temperance, murder, no peace, no love whatsoever and covet thou neighbor's wife.

Ed had it all, accept Sam's wife June especially her. And all of this cause him his demise, for jealousy. Then he tried, his best, to seduce Sheila, which he finally did have his way with her. And she, had to knocked, the hell out of him, to get away from him. Then Jon finished him off, with three slugs into his half man half beast of a body, to end it once in for all. So no one has thought, of Ed, at all. But his daughter, she is trying, to keep his legacy going, in her own way, by being a homicidal maniac like her lunatic dad did, when he was alive. Just a mile and a half away, there is an evil brewing up for an attack on, the Bentford's property. So with evil and destruction getting in gear, to harm, hurt and kill, if necessary,

But Terra and Dana, just wants, what is theirs, a man name Sam Bentford is their prey. As both women, puts a plan in motion, to lured, this man out in, the opening, as a sitting duck waiting to be devoured. As Dana and Terra knows, that the planned has to be very accurate, with no mess ups. Because, grabbing Sam, isn't easy to do, the man maybe old, but he can still hang with the best of them. But with Jon, around, the task becomes difficult, to do. But one thing, both women hasn't figured out is, there are three men in the household. But Sam is the one they need, for a hostage. Why Sam? Since Sam met Terra at Dr. Letchell office. But Sam didn't know, at the time, that Terra was the offspring of Ed's. Ed had talked, to Terra about Sam's life and how Sam mistreated him, when they we're younger. See Ed told, his daughter, how he was mistreated and was done wrong. But he never told, Terra how he never wanted her as a baby, and if he could've, get to a cliff, to through Terra off, he would. Just like he dogged her mother, in which he was going, to kill her. But she died, from cancer, at an early age, afterwards giving birth, to Terra. The Doctor's told, Ms. Terri, that she had a short time, to live. Terri had lung cancer, from cigarettes and pot smoking. Then she became, pregnant by Ed. But Terra ended up in the foster system anyway. Because, Ed's schedule at his auto parts store and he has stolen a Locomotive to committing train killing, for an evil and diabolical way, to do a homicide. The people, that died, was the ones, who hurt Ed some kind of way. But he made sure, that they didn't live long. Now Terra, has that same mentality. Across the cornfield, across the railroad tracks another cul-de-sac near Haskins Rd. That's where this shack sitting, without water, no electricity but a great spot, to lay low. Getting away, from a world of trouble, it seems likely, the other way around, that evil with destruction goes into hibernation isn't heard of. As it always being, that evil seeks, and devoureth. Just like Terra, want quit, until she, gets her man. Another so called, mistake is, that Dana, forgot how Sam looks, because, that day, she was too busy, looking at Jon's rear end. So she, didn't pay any attention, whatsoever, and that the mistake that's going, to lead into problems, for both women.

The very next day, both women, drove pass, the Bentford's home, to see if they can make problems right away. But no one is in sight. So Dana goes down, the road and turn around and come back pass, the house, then they see someone getting into the pickup, to leave. They think it's Sam. As both women look very exciting, to get their man, and put a head cover on him, for not to reveal, their location. As they followed, the pickup, into a store parking lot, to get him and go. Now while Dana has the head cover and gun, in hand, Terra kept, the van running, waiting on Sam, to get out, for to snatch him up. And they struck home. "Whoa." said, the man. As Dana act so aggressive, with, the guy. "If you trying, to remove this cover, I will blow you away, you understand me!?asked, Dana. "Yes" said, the man. As Dana, shoves, the man, into the van, as he just lay there, and not tried, to do anything, to get himself shot. But in his mind, what could he do, to get this kind of treatment. Terra and Dana, kept silence, until they reach, the shack. Then they spoke, to one another. "Get your old ass out, of vehicle!!" Dana, said. "Now! Move it!" said, Dana. "Ok." said, the man. As Terra, went, to get the door, Terra was looking at Dana, with a frustrated look, because, sometime doesn't seem, to look right. To Terra, it looks, like Sam gotten a little taller, with a tommy on him. Dana pushed, the man inside, to the floor, to where he just lying there, and not make a peep. But Terra is still looking at Dana, with a crazy look. Because, Terra is puzzled, with her protégé, thinking who is this under, that head cover. Terra knows, this isn't Sam, because, he wears cowboy boots, this guy has on an expensive work shoe. Terra gave Dana time, to sit, the man up, so that they can talk, with him. But whoever, this is, it's not Sam.

Well minutes later, after Dana had got everything situated, she, then took, the head covering off. "What! Who in the f**k is this!?" asked, Terra. "Sam." said, Dana. "This isn't Sam!!" said, Terra. "Oh wow! We messed up." said, Dana. "No! You messed up!" said, Terra. With a devious stare at her protégé, that she could shoot her, dead in the head, but she isn't going, to do that, they came a long way together, for to destroyed one another. So Dana, stood in front of the man asking who is he. Because both women are definitely confused, and made a big mistake, with their plans exposed, to another individual. But they can't let him go, because he may run, to the law and tell on both women. "My name is Benjamin!" said, Ben. As both women, just stared at the man, don't know, to let him go, or to shoot him. Terra knows, letting him go, is a no no, for him to run, to the authorities. So he's innocent, but still have to die. Because they are exposed, he can go and identified both women. Only biggest secret here is, that they are holding a former cop, in their presence. "So tell me, why are you driving Sam's truck and coming, from his house?" asked, Terra. As Benjamin, uses, his detectives experience, never tell, them exactly the truth, that can compromise, his family in any kind of way. So he plays along, with both women, for not too upset, neither one. Because, both women have a piece of steel in, their hands. But quiet, as kept, Benjamin, notice both of the women, from their mugshots on national t.v. "So why are you two beautiful girls, looking, for Sam?" asked, Ben. "You still haven't, told, me why we're, you driving, his truck and coming, from his house!" said, Terra. As Dana, had put her automatic at Benjamin's throat. "We want, ask you again." said, Dana. "I'm an Insurance Salesman, and Sam is selling he's truck, so he told, me to go and test drive it." said, Benjamin.

"You're an Insurance man!?" asked, Terra. "Yes, so can I sell you both some Insurance?" asked, Benjamin. As both women looking at each other, then started laughing, until Benjamin also laughing, with the women. "Why are you both, laughing at me?" asked, Benjamin. "We are both laughing, because, we want, to kill you, how about that?" asked, Terra. It gotten very quiet and quickly, so Benjamin had to keep, everything, to a minimum, with both women, as Dana tied Benjamin's hand behind his back, and restraints on his feet. Now play time is over, Because Terra is getting ready, to do what she knows, best, and that is throw a tantrum.

Because, she wants, Sam, instead of an Insurance Salesman. Now her attitude is always a little distraught, because, her plans aren't right. "I can't believe, this we have the wrong man!" said, Terra. "Oh sweetheart's, can I be the man, for a day?" asked, Benjamin. "if you don't shut your hole up, you want be talking, for a long time." said, Terra. With her pistol pointed at Benjamin's head. "Sorry, I was just joking." said, Benjamin. "Does it looks like, I want to hear a joke, from you? Huh?" asked, Terra. With all, that was planned, good did once again, prevailed over evil. Because, of her owned lust to harm another, made her and Dana messed up for trying so hard, to get an older guy, like Sam.

As Benjamin, kept, the game going, by compliments to Dana, and letting, her know, that she reminds him, of his ex-wife, back in Hawaii. "You looks just like Sally Jean, my ex-wife of twenty-five years." said, Benjamin. "If she looks like me, man you have good taste." said, Dana. "Hey knock, it off!" Terra, said. "I'm trying, to think, how we can still, get that old bastard, and get rid, of this load of crap!" said, Terra. "Hey buttercup! Why do I have, to be crap?" asked, Ben. Now Terra, sees, the opportunity, to shoot Benjamin, but she needs, to get rid of him, because, he's an innocent bystander, her beef isn't, with him. But he's beef is with both girl's, see his family is being terrorized, by these two individuals, that are armed and dangerous, and kill at will, to solve their hurt. So Ben is trying, his best, to alter, their plans in everyway, from getting to his brother-in-law. To do him harm, and the rest of them, try to keep safe. Now the family is starting, to get a little worried about Benjamin's whereabouts, because, he has been gone, for entire day. But Benjamin is off doing, what he is trained in what matter most is, that preserved life, you may say is far important, then taking a life. To Benjamin, this is a way to negotiate, with a couple of ladies, that is screwed up in the head. That are trying, to be outlaws, and don't have an ideal how to escape, without messing up. Why because, they messed up, trying, to get Sam, instead, they get someone, who wasn't part of their plan, that is a former cop. But too late, not a chance of going backwards, for the two, they have Benjamin now, and he's is putting his expertise, to work. Only one simple problem is, trying to get loose, from his restraints to disarmed, both women, to put them into restraints, then keep them apprehended, unto the authorities come on to the scene.

Now it's two hours, before midnight, and Benjamin isn't back, from, the post office. And Sam, Jon and Sheila are really, to show concerned and a little fear, that something is definitely wrong, for Benjamin, to stay gone, that long. Not only, that, he has the family's truck. But Sheila car is working, if needed. But not the point, that is where could he be? Is the questioned. Sam is starting, to do when June's disappearance came about was to get everybody involved. Like his neighbors up and down, the ways. "Why do I think, that Terra, no good ass, has something, to do, with Uncle Ben's whereabouts?" said Jon. "if she does, I'm going, to shoot, that little whore, in her head, I'm very sick and tired of this woman!" said Sheila. It's getting colder, by the minute, as it getting late also. "Jon, we need, to go by the post officem to see what happened," Sam, said. "At this hour dad?" asked, Jon. "Yes son, now." said, Sam. So all three, Sam, Jon and Sheila, climb into Sheila 's car, to go and look, for Benjamin. Going pass Ed's old house, was a reminder, that his presence is lingering, but only in his one and only offspring, that everyone seems, to not know, to where she could be. Then what a surprise, there're the truck in, the parking lot, with the keys in the ignition, but where is Benjamin's? "What the hell, is going on here!?" ask Sam. As Sheila, stays, in the car, while Jon and Sam, tried to figured out, what and where is Benjamin. "Dad, let's go by, the Sheriff's office. to report this." said, Jon. "I'll drive over there in the truck, while you and sister follow me." Sam, said.

Now they go, to the same jail, where they are holding Cain at. He is incarcerated, waiting on his trial date, to stand and give accountable, for his crimes. Now as the Bentford's arrived, the Sheriff's office looks awfully busy, in trying to catch the other two individual, that are wanted dead or alive. And the law enforcement has a (all-points bulletin) APB, for the two women, to turned themselves in into the law. That's not going, to happened. But Sam, put in a request, to see the Sheriff, but he is holding a meeting, with some of his deputy. But in a nick of time, Sheriff Protzman walks up, to see Sam standing, to see him. They go inside Sheriff Protzman's office to discussed, another disappearance act, this time his brother-in-law. "Sheriff, June's brother is here, staying with for a while, and now he is missing." said, Sam. "Now has it being twenty-four hours, he's being missing?" asked, the Sheriff.

"Ah no, I don't think he has, shucks! I can't recall a darn a thing Sheriff." said, Sam. "Ok, we will, put him on the missing person bulletin."

said, the Sheriff. "Oh one more thing Sheriff, he is a former detective, from Hawaii." said, Sam. "Sam, why didn't he come here, to make his presence known?" asked, the Sheriff. "You know, what this means? He's is one of us." said, the Sheriff. "The law, will step in, to take care and protecting its own." said, Sheriff Protzman. "When was the last time, you seen him? Asked, the Sheriff. "Yesterday Morning, he said, he needed, to go to, the post office, to check on some mail. But the truck was in, the parking lot, with the keys in the ignition, but no sign of him, nowhere, so we were waiting for him to returned, it was an hour, before midnight, still no Ben." said, Sam. "I think, we can get a video recording, from the post office cameras, to see what really had transpired, between when he left, the house and his arrival at the post office." said, the Sheriff.

"Well we intended, to find him, with everything we got and take down, the perpetrator's a.s.a.p." said, the Sheriff. "Sam, we will find your brother-in-law, and if he's a former detective, ain't a darn thing, going to happened, to him, unless he let it." said, the Sheriff. As Sam, leaving, the Sheriff office, hoping, wandering, with an attitude, that he can stomp a hole into someone. This is the same way June's disappearance took place. But only one thing is, that Benjamin is still alive and June's life was taken cause, of envy and jealousy. Again to her husband, his wife didn't deserve to die. Now June's brother is drag into, this curse, so Sam forbidden. Therefore, as a slight repeat of history, trying to show up, but only in a different angle, with a different somebody. Now as Sam getting into his truck, he thought that if Terra, wanted somebody, why didn't she come for him or Jon, instead of Ben. Jon left the car, to check on his father wellbeing, from coming out of the Sheriff office. "Dad, what did Sheriff Proztman say? "asked, Jon. "He said, that they will find him, a.s.a.p." said, Sam. "Dad, I can't believe, this sh**! Is happening again just like mom's situation was!" said, Jon. "I like, to know, too when does, this sh** ends, for someone else die off." said, Jon. "Son let go home, and get out of the cold, I just hope he's ok." said, Sam. "Ok dad, we right behind you." said, Jon.

As the family goes and wait on, the Sheriff office, to make, the first move, in getting a lead on Benjamin's whereabouts, to bring him to safety. But if not, another war, with the perpetrator's, could be devastating, with someone dying on both sides of good and evil. Which is a women's, rebellion against all sides of good. And Terra is, that dictator at the helm of things, just as diabolical as ever. Now the night, has gotten colder, and it's freezing inside of the shack. But with respect, for the women, Benjamin offers, to go and get some wood, to keep warm, but Terra doesn't trust him at all. "Hey Tee, I will go with him, to get some wood, so he won't get a way, from us, without a bullet in his back." said, Dana. "Alright. Keep a close eye on him please!" said, Terra. "If he, looks at you a certain way, you split his wig in half." said, Terra. "And yes! I said, put a bullet in your head, for sure!" said, Terra. Now that all is going on, that Benjamin is taking note at what was said, and their plans with moves. Benjamin, knows, not to let his experience as a detective be exposed, to any criminal, that could get him, a one-way ticket, to heaven. So everything Benjamin is doing is, at low key status. Never let a crook know, that you are on to them. But keep his cover of authority in check. But it's hard, to do sometime, when the criminals are beautiful women, but very diabolical to see, as they are so aggressive, to where you wander if she, gotten, that from her mother or maybe her father.

As Benjamin and Dana goes, to find wood, for the small and ruining fireplace, to get a fire started, for everyone, to be warmed. As both Benjamin and Dana walks, the area around, the shack, that seems, hopeless on a weak foundation, that someday, it may fall, like the evil, that possess it in a previous time. But all though, that Dana did give, the man a lead way in, the dark, to Benjamin knows, that the house isn't far off. But another mistake, that both women, wasn't thinking at all, by letting him walk outside, without a head cover and no restraints. A bad call, with a bad decision by an evil leadership not thinking, that they just jeopardize themselves and compromise, their plans. There was an unusual thing, that only happens so often in the winter, that is thunder snow when a wind is blowing hard, with the snow coming down real hard and its thunder and lightning in the middle of winter. But meanwhile, Dana held her automatic on Benjamin at all times, not letting him close, to her, for any reason at all. As Ben pick up as much as his arms would allow him. While Terra's protégé and hostage, out looking, for wood and logs, for the fireplace Terra is thinking, to herself, how can a plan go so wrong with every detail is plain as simple can go absolutely wrong. As she thought, to herself, that Dana, can be a stupid b**ch at times. And it's all her fault. Terra thought. With self-blameless, Terra thinks, that Terra doesn't do wrong. When Terra shoot someone, it's justified as good, when things aren't going, the way it should, it's wrong. Like in other words getting Benjamin instead of Sam. But getting Benjamin was the right choice, for justices. But wrong for the evil one. It's hurting their plans, for wanting Sam still. But again, the brother-in-law, isn't allowing that, too happened. As the sky, lit up, with lightening as the snow, continuous to fall, with a foot of snow had accumulated within an hours' time. Which no one was going anywhere at all. Meanwhile over the way, the family is so worried about Ben's life, to hoping, that he will show up at home soon of later. But waking up, and getting, that call from, the Sheriff office, to tell, the Bentford's, that Benjamin's body was found in a field nearby, would be a nightmare all over again. As daylight approaches, that everyone is awaken in the Bentfords home. With a lot of tossing and turning and waken up to a miserable day, to see how everything would pan out, in this sinful society, that has nothing to offer, but a cold situation, that is it, for living wrong and dying right. So being on the dark side of things is justified, then being on the light side of thing, which is no fun at all. As civilization gravitates slowly to a dying off society, to where nothing good matter anymore. As you see day after day, how aggressive people has become, no friendliness, no thank you, how are you doing? verses flip you off, get the f**k out of my face! or go to hell! So some people, are immune, to the aggression, then the soft kind words, from the light side of things. This is what people like and love also. But Sam and his family, has chosen, to be their best in keep themselves much humble. And Sam is waiting on, that call from the Sheriff office like the Sheriff did tell him. So Sam is going, to call him at nine o'clock, to get some kind of news, whatsoever.

As Sam finished his breakfast he grabs, the phone, he couldn't no longer, sit and waited. Now Sam sitting at the kitchen table, showing bits of anxious with also obnoxious on the phone with the operator, he just wanted, to know, about his brother-in-laws wellbeing. Before he can run out and kill someone, that tried to harm his family once again. But he already has two people in mind, that is one Terra and two the guys, that came, to the house Nuel and a henchman. So Sam is ready, to do damage. "Hello Sheriff, do you have anything on Benjamin's, whereabouts?" asked, Sam. "No, but we seen, the video who has him." said, the sheriff. "Who? if I may ask. Sam, asked. "Sam, I can't share, that information with you over, this phone." said, the Sheriff. "ok, that all the information, I needed." said, Sam. "Sam, please let us do our jobs, and I don't need, any interference out of you." said the Sheriff. Sheriff Protzman knows, what Sam is capable of getting involved, with the cases, that the law enforcement are working on. In which could get him and his family killed, for interference in a case. But Sam does capitalize on, the situation as quickly as possible, before the other side could counter attack on him and his family. So Sam knows, that the law can be very passive and sloppy on some cases. Like they don't care, because it's not a family member of theirs. But in the meantime, most law agencies, does produce convictions, by building a case against, the defense. For a trial, the case must be solid, for it to stick.

"Hey dad, did, the Sheriff called?" Jon, asked. "No I called him, but they know, what happened. And who has him." said, Sam. "Who!?" asked, Jon. "He wouldn't tell me." Sam, said. "That is a load of bulls**t!" Jon, said. "Yeah, and tell me about it." Sam, said. As Jon and Sam, looked each other in, the eyes like they were reading one another's minds on, this situation about a year and a half ago, this occurs, with June's demised: But the both of Sam and Jon kept things quiet until the very end, to deal, with the perpetrator, for her death. And now it's time, to take it to, the perpetrator's again, without, the Sheriff and his team. As Sheila, comes from her bedroom, to the kitchen. "Morning, hey dad, Jon anything on uncle Benjamin?" Sheila, asked. "yeah, they know, who abducted him, and knows what had happened too." Jon, said. "Who? And don't tell me that idiot Nuel, had something, to do with it." Sheila, said. "we don't know neither, because, that Sheriff Protzman, wouldn't say who." said, Jon. "How in the hell, can someone withhold info, from the family, like that?" Sheila, asked. As Sheila, looks at both her father and brother, to get a response out of one of them. "It's making me feel disgusting" said, Sheila. So Sheila just left the kitchen without another word mention Going back, to her room, and thinking a lot about Cain wellbeing. He's is somewhere safe, from this situation, but Cain, will be out in no time. But if the Judge determines, his fate, he could be incarcerated, for a long time. All though, he did murder another man, for spitting on him. But Cain didn't mean, to kill anyone. Cain has a slight temper, that he is trying his best, to put in check. Like before it's hard to be humble.

At some point in life, the brain and heart are the two vital organs, that works together. But the tongue is a vital and deadly muscle, that can't be tamed. The heart tells, the brain, to have the tongue, to curse, that man out, and that's what happens, when people, let their heart lead them or follow your heart. See Cain, had a hard time, believing, that he had kill someone. Before his incarcerated, Cain thought, he was in a nightmare. Cain commit a real homicide, which makes him a felony, with also a first offense. But the courts don't care about a first offense, to the courts, the judge needs a pending trial, to prove an innocent man didn't mean, to killed another. But if Cain does, his time, maybe he could get out on good behavior. That if he wants, to see Sheila again ever, like he said, he wants, to have Sheila hand in marriage. But Sam, thinks it's too soon, to be talking about marriage between both Cain and Sheila.

A Sinister's Visit

Chapter VIII

As Jon and Sam, both sitting at the kitchen, table thinking on how they can handle, this situation on their own. Like they did before, be as discretional as much as possible, with only one another. While discussing their little plans, there was a strange knock at the door, a knock, that they never heard before. Jon looks out the window, and it's a deputy cruiser in front of the house. Jon opened, the door in a hurried, thinking that the deputy has some news, on Benjamin. Sam came quickly, to the door as well. With the deputy stepping inside of the house. "Good morning Mr. Bentford, the Sheriff needed for me to come and check on you and your family, to make sure, that you all are ok." said, the deputy. "Are you, f**ken for real!?" asked, Sam. "I don't believe this!" said, Jon. "Yes sir, he did." said, the deputy. "Well you go back and tell, Eugene, that we are ok, what a sorry man he is, and I don't know why we voted, to put him in office, no good muth*&%^er!" said, Sam. "i will, you folks enjoy the rest of your day." said the deputy. As the deputy, was leaving out, there comes Sheila out of her room," Hey what was all the yelling about?" asked, Sheila. "We can believe, that Sheriff Protzman, would send a darn deputy, to see if we were ok." said, Jon. "What!?" Sheila, asked. "Yeah" Jon, said. "I'm tired, of waiting, they did, the same with your mother's disappearance, if Protzman, thinks, that I'm going to wait any longer, he is sadly mistaken." Sam, said. "It be a cold, day in hell, if we waited on Sheriff Protzman." Sam, said. "I'm still thinking, on how come, they can't tell us who abducted, Uncle Benjamin, if it's for money, they would've call by now, because, why wouldn't they asked for any demands, it doesn't seem right, with him being abducted like that." said, Jon. "Something isn't right about this situation, at all." Sam, said. As snow cover everything in its path, it looks like, the area is paralyzed. Because, some are stuck and can't go anywhere, unless they dig their way out. Meanwhile Benjamin is trying his best in entertaining, these dangerous women and keeping everyone warm, until he can figure out where exactly he is at to make a move. But Dana, has her weapon constantly on Ben's every move. While Terra, keeping her distance, from all the snow and anything with water, can make her itch real bad and messes, with her powers.

Just like her, father had went through, the same situation, whenever he's around water. Because, evil doesn't want anything, to do with cleanliness, water represent purification, with evil in control, there's no good, no good, no cleanliness So that evil is allergy, to cleanliness. That's why she couldn't be in a nice hotel, with Jon, at the time, somewhere dark and filthy and no running water, isn't allowed. Now that's very suitable, for a person like Terra and her accomplices, to lay low, from the authority, and the dirt and evil, they have done. But Benjamin is still playing, their game, as long as it takes, to wear, them down, to apprehended both ladies. But he needs, to think very hard into getting, that weapon out of the hands of Dana. And how, to escape, without being harm. With Ben's experience can handle both women, but when one is watching his every move, can be a difficult task. So he acts nonchalant, about everything, until he could get a grip on his whereabouts, to make a certain move, for a distraction, to get the gun out of Dana's hands. But he knows, it's all about perfect timing, to catches everyone off guard. With this shack, always dark inside, was a task, to see what's happening in front of him. And there's a lock on the door, to keep things, from leaving out and a small window, that hold a little sunlight. The place was a mess and it stinks every moment. Because, if you need, to relieve yourself, you would go to the corner of the shack, to do whatsoever, you need to do. This shack was a perfect for holding hostage.

This place is where Ed, took in his hostages and kept them for days on edge. He would bring them here and did some of everything, to them. Especially the women. Yeah! He would, be very dirty towards, the women here no one can hear you scream out here. And he also murdered, some of his victims here too. The very thing, that surprised, the surrounding communities, was that, the law, has come up on this place, a million times, and never offered, to stop and see if things were right at all. But they can show up at the Bentford's place, with a weird piece of news, that everyone is already aware of. So if the law enforcements were concerned about protecting and preserved life, they could've save many lives, from this location, if they would tear it down, to keep things, from getting any worst, then they are. But the locals knew, of Ed, but not so much of his business. Because, Ed did keep his personal business very discretional, from the public eyes. But some definitely knew, far in the background was an evil mass, that couldn't be revealed. But if reveal, it was a matter of time, before Ed, would cross your path, to bring about someone's, anyone's demised. Someway somehow, you were rid of. Now that Ed is, gone forever, his daughter is his infamous legacy, that she must pick up, from where Ed, has left off, but she must understand, that she also will fall like him, when the time approaches.

As Benjamin is still, trying to pinpoint, the direction, the shack is sitting, which he doesn't know, that the house is, in walking distances, from where he is at, but what direction, would he run in. So Terra, approaches Benjamin, to let him go, so that they still need, Sam as a hostage. "Hey man, I'm letting you go, because you are getting on my last nerve. I need Sam, still, and there's nothing stands in my way." Terra, said. But Benjamin, tried, to convince Terra, to keep him instead of going after his brother-in-law. But Benjamin, must move very quickly, or his brother-in-law could, be a victim, to these savvy, homicidal maniac women, who will kill at a drop of a dime "No keep, me please, I love you women, I think you both are so cool, at what you are doing, I never being in a women gangster's way." Ben, said. "Wow! I like you very much." said, Dana. "Now we are women gangsters? Asked, Terra. While both women chuckle a bit. "You are a very flattery person Benjamin! But flattery doesn't, feed us, Sam does." said, Terra. So why, should we keep you? You aren't our problem, Sam is, so go back to selling insurance." said, Terra. "I tell you what, if you both need a man, to help around here, just say so, and I would stay, for a while, c'mon what you say." said, Benjamin. As both women, talk among each other in the other room, so Benjamin, couldn't hear a word, they were saying, but it had to be bad, for them to travel to, the other room. But as both women left, to goes, to the room, Ben tried, to see if he could get out of his restraints, but Dana made quite sure, the insurance salesman, wasn't going anywhere just yet. As both women come over, to offer Benjamin a proposition, in helping, them in getting Sam, for their hostage.

But Benjamin, was very shock, to hear them asked him, to do somethings like that, would be, a battle, that couldn't happen' if he said, yes. Now both women, are so in trouble, that they asking a former law officer, to kidnapping, his own flesh and blood, to turn him over, to them. Benjamin, knows, that the two women, has really lost their minds. But if Benjamin, had told, both women, that he is Sam's brother-in-law, he wouldn't be breathing, so he need, these two killers, to play his game, a little longer. But the women, are determines, to get Sam some kind of a way and Benjamin, is trying to hold'em off, with a story, that might change, their mines. "Hey ladies, listen, I heard, that there are two guys, looking for you two women, I don't know, who they are, but they do want you two women really bad, So the law is looking, for you both and also two guys are on your tails too." said, Ben. "What guys!? Are looking for us?" asked, Dana. "Hey you better not be lying, to us!" said, Terra. "What in the heck, is two guys, want with us? "asked, Terra. "Do you know, what they look like?" asked, Dana. "For as I know, that we went, to a mansion, and clean house, and that house, belongings, to a gangster, by the name of Nuel. And he is dead also with all of his henchmen's." said, Terra. As both women, boasting about a mass homicide, that they both had done, to a former cop, isn't too smart, to do. Everything they are saying, will be used in court, that if it makes it to court. "I swear, they called the both of your names." said, Benjamin. Now Benjamin has both ladies, where they need to be, there in deep thought, on who's looking for them. Benjamin has the ladies, confused, on what's what, and the shack has gone quiet, for a moment, with them thinking, to themselves. Until now they both are paranoid. Because, all of the homicides, they both had committed, but maybe missed, two of the guys, that was at Nuel's place.

Now a mountain of problems starts, to manifest, for the killer duo, because, they made it plain, to others, about their business. They couldn't keep their mouths shut, neither couldn't be somewhat discretion. The thing, with Ed, was a loner and did his crimes, by himself, without accomplice. That's what made him different, then his daughter, a girl with another female accomplice, that runs her mouth a lot and making very terrible mistakes, without thinking at all. And for the leader, she leaves everything on another person, so when things not according, to her standard, then it's their fault. But when stuff is going in the wrong direction it's everybody fault still. But when a killing is taking place, she is just as happy with herself, plain and simple. So if these women, think, that Benjamin, would hands, his brother-in-law over, to them, they are so sadly mistaken, they are beautiful women, without a conscience and not one morals about herself. They were at one time a great girl, to be around, but she has a despicable walk with her evil talk, until the whole world, would come under her silhouette of damnation, because, she was forsaken by men in general. But to bad baby, you pass yourself off, as equal, to a man. Not understanding, that she orders her steps as a criminal too. But one man, she could be mad at, that's her father, who's gene, that was pass on to her. Ed was a miserable man, that hasn't held a woman in years. Because, his evil ways wouldn't allow him, to be a good man. When he made a bargain, with the devil, it can alter, the appearance and ego, his ways of thinking and doing things. No more of you or yourself.

But meanwhile, the Bentford's home is feeling very tense inside, over Benjamin's whereabouts. Now it's being forty-eight hours, since, they heard anything else, from the Sheriff office. It's ashamed, to get something done, when you always have to do it yourself, by getting involved in which is so wrong. Because, the innocent is the one end up dead somehow, So Jon and Sam, getting ready, to go hunting, for Benjamin, to get him back. It may take a moment, but he's back at home where he belongs. As Sheila, watches her father and brother take off, to look, for Ben, as she stays in, from the cold. By her staying home, could be a mistake, with two individual watching, the house. When Jon and Sam pull out of the driveway they headed west and the two individuals came, from the east as they continue, to scope, the house out, before pulling into the driveway. But they saw, both father and son leave, so why are they going, to the house? They needed, to speak, with Sheila, for a moment. One of the individuals got out and goes, to see if Sheila is inside, he knocks on the storm door, to see if she would open, the door. Sheila was in her bedroom, and she heard, the knocking, but was skeptical about seeing who it was and opening, to some stranger. So she goes and lookout to see who it is, the minute she saw who it is, she hesitated in opening, the door, to hear whatsoever Nuel had to say. "Hey I know, you are in there, please! I have some interesting news for you, about your precious Cain." said, Nuel. Sheila, open the door slightly, to hear whatever, the gangster had to say.

"What in the world man, you have to tell me?" asked, Sheila. "About your boy Cain, he isn't good, for you." said, Nuel. "Why would you say that?" asked, Sheila. "That woman, she, had shot me in, the shoulder, for what? I will never know." said, Nuel. "Why! Did she, shoot you, and who was it, that shot you?" asked, Sheila. "That crazy b**ch! Terra was her name! And, that other woman, took my money." said, Nuel. "So what does, this have to do, with Cain?" asked, Sheila. "Cain, was one of her accomplices." said, Nuel. "What!! you have, to go." said, Sheila. "I just wanted, to enlightening, you about who you are getting involved with." Nuel, said. "Well you done enough." Sheila, said. As Sheila closes, the door, with a little furious on her side, she is thinking of hurting someone or herself. But she doesn't want do that, so when she, ever see Cain, she will ask him, about himself. But also Sheila's thoughts, is not to believe, what she just heard, from a rogue individual, like Nuel. Who is out, to seek all kinds, of revenge on anybody and everybody? As Nuel, planet, the seed as he thought, to ruin it for Cain, being with Sheila. But the far and worst is yet, to come, when Cain, finds out, that Nuel, paid Sheila, a visit and why. Though Cain maybe lock up, but he still may get out early on good behavior. But Nuel is, vowed to get both women, and will not stop until he has them both in his hands. But for Sheila is, wandering in curiosity, on how much does Nuel knows, but not saying at all, about Cain's involvement with Terra. As she, sat on the side of her bed, thinking it's more to the story, then he's leading her on too. Why hear him out, that may have something, to do with uncle Benjamin's disappearance. Sheila thought. Meanwhile Sam and Jon are riding around, looking for something, to shoot, that may look suspicious, to them, to have a reason, to give a shot. On their, way back home, Sam wanted, to stop at Ed's old home, for a hunch, to see if Benjamin is there or not. Jon pulls, the truck up in, the driveway of, the house, they both had their weapons at hands, Sam looks inside, to see if his brother-in-law, to see if he's in sight anywhere. As both men walk, throughout the house looking for clues, that could lead them, to Benjamin's whereabouts. The house, had a heavy stench, with trash everywhere you turned, with mices running everywhere. "Man! What a dump, this is!" said, Jon.

Now as the weather shift, to cloudy and cold, both men were trying, their best in finding Benjamin's whereabouts, as they returned, for tomorrow, to see if any luck. But before, they can get out of the door of, Ed's old house, they seen a female's garment, that looks like it could be Terra's. Because, both Sam and Jon, has seen her, in that particular garment, so she, couldn't denied not having it. But it does, prove she was there. The front door, was unlocked and the bedrooms, was also trashed. It stinks, like an animal live here as well. But Jon knows, that Ed, was part man and part beast. "There's one more place, we need, to check, and that's the basement." Sam, said.

"Wait a minute dad, let me get, the flashlight out of, the truck, Please." Jon, said. "Ok son, hurry." said, Sam. As Jon when and returned, with the flashlight, to enter into, the basement, with it being as dark, without lights, would be impossible, to see a thing. So as going into, the basement, there were a different stench, as they reach, the floor of the basement, and as both men started, to feel sick, to their stomachs, there was two piles of human remains in the corners of the basement, to where Ed had a couple down here, for hostages. "Dad I can't take this smell, anymore." said, Jon. "I think, we should, report this." said, Sam. "Dad, wait a minute! How are we, going to report, this? When we shouldn't be here." said, Jon. "Son I guess you are absolutely right, let's go." said, Sam. "That Ed, was a very sick individual, I tell you, good riddens." said, Sam. The minute, that Jon hit the air, outside he regurgitates, from that unpleasant odor of death in a basement. So both men didn't realize, that they have visit, the graves of the two individuals in Ed's basement, are now a tomb, for those two individuals. "After seeing that, we need to find, uncle Benjamin, fast and quick." said, Jon. Now it dark and cold out, the men, will start early morning, if still not a word, from Sheriff Protzman office, In which Sam, do take offense too, being lied too. All Sheriff Protzman ever do is tell the public, what he wants, them to hear. Just as a political leader does, and people take offence, to the matter. Well Sam isn't falling for the lied too scheme of things, but to do it themselves is alright, with them. At least, the job is started, to the finished, that's the Bentford's way. By not waiting on, the Sheriff office, and investigating, things themselves could be very risky, Because, lives are at stake and the authority are looking for two fugitives still, and one is already incarcerated, and with the two women at large, and a gangster, on their tails, would be a mess soon or later. And Benjamin Tills, and Bentford's, are all part of, the abyss of trouble.

Now that, the night has come, and gone, Sam is cooking breakfast, for the family, as everyone is get up, to get their day going: Sheila, comes to the kitchen, with a disappointed look and a slight attitude, because, she felt a bit of betrayal by her friend Cain. "Morning honey." said, Sam. "Morning Dad, I'm so sorry dad, I should've, listen to you." Sheila, said. "Well why?" asked, Sam. "Well while you and Jonny, was gone, that guy Nuel, showed up, with some news, that I didn't care, to hear." Sheila, said. "Well what did he say?" asked, Sam. As she being very hesitant in telling her, father, in what he needs, to know, what Nuel, had told, her about Cain. "Nuel said, that Cain is an accomplice of Terra's." said, Sheila. "All s**t!" Sam, said. "So now I might, have to shoot him too!?" asked, Sam. "Sweetheart, tell him, that he isn't allowed here anymore ever." said, Sam. "Morning! Why all, the yelling and long faces?" asked, Jon. "Do you want to tell, your brother, what you, just told, me?" asked, Sam. "Tell me what!?" asked, Jon. "Nuel, came over yesterday, and said, that Cain is accomplice for Terra." said, Sheila. "Now do we have to shoot him?" ask, Jon. "i said, the same thing." said, Sam. "But what if he's trying, to change his ways, and being a better man?" asked, Sheila. "Sheila, he will always going, to be bad, and besides he was running with our adversary." said, Jon. "Have you forgot, that Terra is like her, old man, and still at large, I be glad, when the authority, catch, that evil old b**ch!" said, Jon. "Why do I have a hunch, that darn woman has something, to do with Benjamin's disappearance?" asked, Sam.

"By the way, Dad any news on uncle Benjamin's situation?" asked, Jon. "Not yet son." said, Sam. "So are we still going, to look, for him, or what?" asked, Jon. "Yup, But I have an an ideal, we are going, to the bowling alley, library and post office, to look around, to see if anyone willing, to talk, to us." said, Sam. While everyone, was in the kitchen talking and discussing on what to do, for the day, everyone heard, that familiar sound, that had everyone running, for cover, that is a sound of a locomotive coming up, the tracks. And it is, coming fast, with not two, but six locomotives pulling, with millions of tons, of freight and cargo. As Sam and Jon stood at the back door, looking at the train go by. As Sam thought, that Ed, would come and tried, to start some more mess, but realized, that Edward Dart, will never returned in this lifetime he is, gone forever. Just like June, never will I see her warm and lovely face again. Sam thought. As Sam, tried, to hold back his tears, for thinking about someone who is so precious to him, that left this planet, so soon, and leaving a mark in all of their hearts. Sam thought.

As Sam and Jon, were getting ready, to go: Sam was looking a little red in, the face, but he grabs his, chest. "Dad! hey are you ok?" asked, Jon. As Sheila, grabs, the phone, to dial, the emergency line, to get a paramedic. While Jon, helps his father, to the sofa, and waited on, the paramedics, to come. "I felt a little light headed, then the pain up my arm wow." Sam, said. "Dad, just take it easy, the paramedics is on it way so stay still." Sheila, said. "By the way, did you take your meds this morning?" asked, Sheila. "I can't remember, sweetie." said Sam. "Dad, here's the paramedics." Sheila, said. "Hi c'mon in and he's over there." Sheila, said. "Hello, I'm going, to ask, you a few questions ok?" asked, the medic. "Are you on any meds? Are you lightheaded now? And did you eat this morning?" asking, the medic. As Sam, answer all question's lying down. While the paramedics checking his vitals, someone else is also, checking things out, from across, the way. Terra has notice, that a paramedic van is in front of the house, with her eyes, like her fathers, she can see, things like an eagle would see them, like as prey. As the paramedics, put Sam on, the gurney, to take him, to Lajunta Memorial, for to be treated. Sam was experiencing, a mild heart attack, it kinda, put his, left arm, in a hanging mode. But he is still alive, from someone prayers. As Jon and Sheila, headed also behind, the EMS as it transported, their dad, to the hospital. But not far along, is Dana, on the tail, to find out where are they going in, the ambulance, and who is in, the ambulance? So Dana, will be the eyes, for her boss, Terra. See the

Bentford's recognized, Terra, when they see her, But Dana, they don't know, So Dana stay's close, to cover, their every move. The EMS pulls into, the emergency section, to take Sam onto, the Intensive care unit, to be treated. While Dana is, watching their every move, Terra is, man sitting, Benjamin, as he sits and being restraints, to a chair, for hours, without any food, no running water, to drink, and he needs, to relieve himself. But Benjamin is, willing to play the game, even longer, if needed. A man, that is definitely, loves his family, wouldn't mind at all, going the distance, whatsoever it takes. Most men will put their family at risk, for not being as close, to home. But instead of making peace, and negotiate. They do somethings very stupid, like not thinking in what they are saying. Because, either, they are too scared, to man up, for his family. Or just not come, to terms, and died off. With Benjamin's experience in, the professional level of law enforcement is, working, to its advantage, by keeping his suspects at arm's length, and not a chance, for a getaway. Just how ironic, for the suspects, to landed into a former cop lap. And not know it. Ben knows, if he could get a loose, to wrestle with Terra, and take her glock 34, from her, and put her into restraints, to hold her until the Sheriff department arrived. And Dana, keeps her glock 26, at her side, at all times. So Benjamin doesn't have a chance, to show, the ladies, what he can work with. Because, Benjamin is, trying to leave unharmed and while protecting what matters most is his family. But if he can also serve as a retired veteran cop, doing what he knows best is good, and already protecting, that is so precious, to him is good also. Last but least, if he can preserve, the two women lives, he would probably be ask, to joined Sheriff Protzman's department. So he did, everything, that the force, has taught him, to uphold the law, and serve, and protect, and preserved life.

So with, Benjamin held hostage, Terra is, keeping a close eye on him and wandering, when and if, she will have Sam in her hands, soon enough; with Dana's report on where, they are keeping him in, the hospital. Then it would, be a glorious day, that Sam was delivered into her hands, after all. But the way, things are looking, that Terra, may have both men as her hostages. Because, once Dana, has returned, with the news, that Terra would be hoping for, to go and bring Sam's butt back, to the shack. As waiting, for Dana, to get back, the place was quiet, because, Terra, has gag Benjamin's mouth, to keep him quiet, for a moment, so Terra can think on her, next step, once Sam is there, so kill Benjamin, then send Dana, to closed, the curtains on Jon and Sheila and burned, the house down, with them inside. This is no way, to describe how far evil can go, to destroyed another life and the thing is they didn't give, a life, for to take a life. That's the problem, with an evil parasite making choices, and calling decisions within, but that's the wicked nature of, having an entity inside of an evil one. Most had Terra's thought, of killing Benjamin and goes, to exterminate all of the Bentford's, and then leave town. It seems, that the little witch, has being busy thinking of advancing, her plan's, for to move on, from where she is. Now the nurses, are prepping Sam, for the doctors, to look at him, while they are getting, the information, from Jon and Sheila, while Sam, just lying comfortable on the bed. As Dana, has shown up, to keep her eyes on, the prize, and get the info, from a nurse if needed. Dana as she is, sitting in the visitors waiting room, waiting on Jon and Sheila, to come out. As Sheila and Jon, comes, to sit, and wait, for the doctors, to let them know, what's going on, with their father's health. But while, Jon and Sheila, was conversing, with each other, as Sheila looks over, at Dana, and finds Dana gazing at her, for whatever reason; "Excuse you! Can I help you!?" ask, Sheila. "No I think, you are the one, that needs, help, after I whip your ass!!" said, Dana. "Hey Sheila, who is that? asked, Jon. "I don't know, but she better, stop looking at me, before I give her a blackeye!" said, Sheila. "Sheila, just ignored her, please she looks like, that girl on, the wanted poster." said, Jon. When Jon, had mention, that she looks like, the girl on, the wanted poster, Dana left, the waiting room, staring at Sheila, as she exits out, with an attitude. "Jonny I don't know, that b**ch, from Eve!" said, Sheila. See Dana, was smart, and not so smart, her ideal, was to induce a fight, with Sheila on, the spot for to get them kick out of, the hospital, so

Terra and herself can get Sam, for themselves. But it didn't work As evil tried, to prevailed, with getting Sam out of, there later on, tonight. But they need, for Sheila and Jon, to leave, so no interference comes, from them, at all. It seems, to be problem, getting Sam, because, security is heavy all over, the place, Well people, can thank Sheila, for that, Because, after Ed, had removed Sheila, from her room, a year ago, the hospital tightens security big time.

As Dana, getting ready, to leave the hospital, to report back, to her boss and girlfriend, to give her some disappointed news. And she knows, that Terra doesn't, like bad news, because, when it comes, to getting what she, deserve, Terra is like every bit of her father. If Ed is, going, to kill someone, he makes a way, to get you, and nothing stands in, the way. Well Terra, will absolutely do the same. But before she can leave, Dana goes, to a nurse, and lied about being a daughter of Sam. So she could have some information on his room and what's next, for him. But the nurse told, her that she would have to wait on, the doctor, to speak, with him. The nurse couldn't tell her anything. "F**k!" said, Dana. In a frustrated mood, Dana, goes, to the waiting room, to give Jon and Sheila, her middle finger, as she was leaving. "Sheila! Come back here, will you?" asked, Jon. "Hey b**ch! Come on, let's do this, so I can take your finger, and stick it up your own ass!!" Sheila, said. "Man! Why is this woman, acting this way, towards us?" asked, Jon. "Yeah! That's what, I thought!" said, Sheila. "I hope, to God, that I will see, that heifer again!" said, Sheila. As a nurse, approached both Jon and Sheila, to see, if everything was ok, then she asked, if their sister, was alright. Both Sheila and Jon, thought that was a joke coming, from the nurse. "What! That woman, isn't no way in hell, related, to us." said, Jon. "Sorry, she said, that she was Sam's daughter." said, the nurse. "No! we are, the only two offspring he has, so far, but really, that woman isn't with us, and she tried, to start trouble, with us as well, for whatever reason." said, Jon.

"Wait, so she said, that she is his daughter?" asked, Sheila. "That's what, she just told, us, and she wanted, his room number, then I said, we don't have that information yet, then she started, to curse." said, the nurse. "Nurse, can you get the authorities here?" asked, Jon. "I'll do better, then that, I'll call, our security team." said, the nurse. As both Jon and Sheila, standing and talking among, themselves, about Dana a mysterious woman, just coming out of nowhere, to start trouble is, a little ridiculous. "Hi can I help you folks?" asked, the security guard. "Sorry to bother you, but we just had a mysterious woman, coming here, to claim, that she is our father's daughter, and we don't know, and we are, the only children, he has, So we don't know this woman, at all." said, Jon. "She just started, with my sister, for nothing, and she, came inside, the waiting area, to give us a middle finger, then she left." said, Jon. "I said, to myself, what is that for?" Jon's thought. "Well if she comes back here again, we will have her arrested." said, the security guard. "I believe, we can pull, the video, to see what had happened, and turn it over, to the authorities." said, the security guard. "You don't mind, what's your father's name?" asked, the security guard. "His name is, Samuel Bentford." Jon, said. "This here, would allow us, to place, a guard on his room, around the clock, to protect him, from whoever." said, the security guard. "Thank you, that is great, to know, and our father, will definitely appreciate it, so again thank you so much." Sheila, said. Now with, that protection, could make it very difficult, for Terra and her accomplice, to remove Sam, from his room. But anybody and everybody does know, how evil shall work, to accomplished whatever it needs, without any interference. But the accountability of wrong doing is, sometimes a little confusing and also misleading, the public, that things will be as is, for a trial, once the women are capture. For Cain, there isn't any hope, for him. Because, his DNA was all over, the crowbar he uses, to slay, the sheriff deputy. Cain left, the evidence, next to porch in the backyard of, Ed Dart's house. So Cain may not see, his love interested not ever, if a jury and judge determines his fate. And before, that his beating the death of a man, for spitting on him, for refusing, to buy, the man a beer. The Judge, Jury and prosecutor, may exempt, the charges. Because, Cain had a couple of, witnesses, that saw what happened. But for him, to escape, a group home, was a light sentence of two years in Lajunta correctional facility, And the Judge, dare him, to escape again, for a hefty sentence as Cain, stands, before the Judge, to accepted his sentences for his wrong doings, but he knows, it a season, to come clean, and man up, about his mistakes and remained content under, the care of the law once again. But finally, Cain is a man of change and seeking, to do better, with his life, for to move forward. Cain feels, very awkward being in a cage like an animal, being trap and can't breathe. But he knows, for sure, that two years, isn't very long in a positive note, then doing twenty years in comparison. Therefore, Cain has accepted his dirty deeds, that made him, to consumed, county colors, with a number and the restrictions, that goes alone, with the address of justice, not for all. As the bailiff, places Cain, into his cell, where he walks in and sat down, on his cot, to get used to it, and sort of comfortable too.

But he has, a matter, to content with, and that is, Sheila, being on his brains, trying to hold on, and think positive things, as the days get longer, and nights shorter, as Cain's mind, started to run back and forth in running again. But the judge's ruling is stuck in his head, as well, about running again, that his sentences is a hefty one, if he decides, to run. So Cain, will remember, the judges saying, for in order, to see Sheila again. Cain must, take a stance, and do right, so he can get back, to Sheila. But when it's all said, and done, Cain has to clear, his situation up, with Sheila, about his involvement, with Terra, as accomplice. This doesn't sit well, with Sheila, of course. And for Sam, doesn't want, to see Cain, with his daughter, at all, But it doesn't matter, what he wants, it all about his daughter's wellbeing, and keeping her happy.

A Capitalize Situation

Chapter IX

Now that Dana, has returned, to give Terra, a report, about the hospital, and Terra was so distraught, on good news. But she was glad, to have some news, that Sam is, in the place, for her to go and get. Terra, already has a disguise, to get Sam. She will play a nurse, to Sam, like she did before, she started her murdering of Dr. Letchell and his staff. But she isn't going, to kill Sam yet. But she may kill, Benjamin first, for spoiling, their plans, for being in, the wrong place and the vehicle, at the wrong time. As Dana, was telling, Terra, that she, couldn't get the room number, because, "Sam was still in, the ICU nit. But I did run into that darn, Sheila and Jonny, they are there, in the waiting room." said, Dana. As both women, were standing in, the other room discussing how they were going, to get Sam, but wasn't aware, that Benjamin, heard every word, that was discussed among them. So he, started yelling, about his legs, has no feeling, both women, came, to see what the deal was, and why Benjamin was yelling. All Benjamin, was causing, a diversion, to buy, some time, to get a loose, to knock, the hell out of both women, if he can. But his restraints, were, a little tight on his wrist, and his ankles are tape, to the legs of the chair. As one of the women, check his restraints, why the other, held him, at gun point. So Benjamin knows, not to tried anything, to get a hole put in him, not to give, them any reason, to shoot him, Benjamin, thought. As Benjamin, stood up, to stretch his legs, for the blood, to flow. "Man! I hate being old!" said, Benjamin. "i can, put you out of, your misery, if you like, if not, sit your ass back, down in this chair." Terra, said. As Benjamin sat down slowly, he notices, there is, a slight change in Terra's appearance. Her eyes were different colors, with her hair, grew a bit longer, and her skin tone, had a slight odor, to it. Not to mention, her nail started, to look like, a baby eagle's talons. Then and there, Benjamin knew, that this woman, was like her father. The way that, his family described, Ed's evil side. But Benjamin, had, to use some sense of humor, with Terra looking more and more of, a she monsters. "Wow, you look good honey. "Benjamin, said. "Are you being, very sarcastic? because, your flattery, will get you killed here." Terra, said. "Sorry, I was just, giving you a complement woman, didn't mean any harm." said, Benjamin. "Well I don't want your, complement's, I really want, to kill you, that's what, I want." Terra, said. "Really, you want, to kill a man, for complementing your butt, wow! What has this world come too?!" asked, Benjamin. "A person like me, doesn't do complements, I believe, that a complement got us all here." Terra, said. "Hey! You need, to light up, a bit, from being so evil, why be evil, and you may do some good someday." said, Benjamin. "No way in hell, why would I do that?" asked, Terra. "It's so annoying, very irritating, to me, so don't give me, that bull, about doing good, because, I have a chance, to run, for Sheriff, with all the killings, I done." said, Terra. Then and there, Benjamin's thoughts, that there is, a serious insult, to law enforcement everywhere, for her to say something, like that. "for that comment, I wish, I could slap her in her mouth, for that. "Benjamin's thought. And again, both women, not knowing, everything they say or do, Benjamin is, keeping everything in mind. As Terra, acts snotty, about being good, Benjamin is working his restraints, to where he is getting a loose. So he can get, to safety. He can handle one, but both at the same time, can be a little extreme, especially, with a gun in her hands. Benjamin knows, to smooth talk, the women into letting him stay with them, to keep, them from getting to his brother-in-law. If the women were let on, that he's a former detective in any kind of way, Terra will, do execution style on, the former and retired detective, with a little, assistance from Dana. This is Dana's specialty in killing, a person. Before Dana, was Dana, she had, a good man, that was ready, to married her, but he couldn't hold his liquor, and couldn't keep his manhood in his pants.

So on a hot night, Gerald decides, to get drunk, and bring, a young harlot, to the house, that him and Dana had plan, to make, a home with. Gerald was so drunk, he forgot what day and time it was, which Dana, was a restaurant manager, full of ambitious, and a lot of potential in coming, a restaurant owner. But her envy, jealousy, and lasciviousness conduct made her, into a female monster, and she lost everything, she worked for, and gave her life, to become a killer. The night, that Dana, was supposed, to be at work, she decides not, to report, to work, that night. Dana, went, to the mall, to buy Gerald, a birthday gift, with his birthday in another week. Dana had gotten, Gerald, a gold necklace and bracelet set, that she knows, he would love it. As happy, as she was, getting that for the man she loves, but at times, Dana knows, loving Gerald, was a great thing. But he never shows, Dana that he loves her back. But that night, was supposed to be a special occasion. Instead, that night, had turned very deadly and quick. Dana comes home, to Gerald and one of his whore's, he knew back in the day, in bed together. Dana was so hurt, she didn't make, a sound, standing in the doorway of their bedroom. While Gerald, was inside of the harlot, with both doing heavy breathing, they didn't hear Dana come in, or hear her in the doorway. As Dana, goes without any hesitation to her hall closet, and get her toy, and that is her glock 26 and then returned, to her bedroom, to dispose human bacteria and waste, at the same time. As she cried, and close her eyes, to do something, she thought, she wouldn't never do. That was, to put Gerald and, the harlot, to sleep, while they both were caught up in, the moment, before Gerald can cum inside, and the harlot climax, Dana puts two in each one's head, then she, walked and left everything.

It was, a full month, before anyone notice, that Gerald was missing, in action. But a mail carrier has notice, a loud stench coming, from the home. So he cares enough, to call, the authority, to see what's up, with the residences, and the mail is piling up, all over the porch. The authority, had to investigated, the scene, to nail, who did, what to the two individuals, and the finger is pointing in Dana Lynn direction. Because, Dana is, the number one suspect, with leaving, all evidences, the door knob, her name and Gerald's name, are on pieces of mail, and when she killed, Gerald and the harlot, neighbors said, that they heard gun shots coming, from the residences, with Dana coming out minutes later, to leave. Therefore, that's why Dana love, to execution her victims, with a surprise, from the back. The correctional institution is trying, to get Dana back, for her trial day is soon, if the authorities can apprehend her soon. The case of, the restaurant shooting and killing of, the father and his five sons, her fiancée Gerald's and the harlot. These are the cases, that are pending, against Dana Lynn, if she helps her boss and girlfriend, to kill Sam and his brother-in-law, this case, would impending along, with the others. But Benjamin is on the job, by keeping, things in check, with a pair of dangerous women, who is making, a move on his lovable family. But Benjamin is trying, to make a move himself by getting a loose, if he needs to shoot one, then oh well, it is, what it is, because, they would shoot him, if they had, the chance to do so. But meanwhile, Terra is disguising herself very well, to concealed her identification, from the public and from her enemies. With a simple, wig and some makeup, and a mini skirt will set the tone, to relieve any man mind when they look at her, for that desired lust. Terra knows, that a man, can have a strong appetite, for a woman, with a big behind and hips, and a deadly smile is, behind it all.

Both Terra and Dana, are determined, to get Sam, and bring him back, and have Dana, to use her execution style on Benjamin, when he isn't expecting it. As Benjamin, see that both women, do mean business, and nothing isn't going, to stand in their way. Now Terra sees, what goes around, comes around also. Maybe an eye, for an eye. But her thought is, this, a father, for a father, Terra's thought. Now she's thinking even does make it right. But evil, for evil, makes things much more wicked. Like good, for good, equals merciful and understanding, as people, with humility, shows kindness, and meekness see things through, a different lens on life. When wickedness, doesn't see, because, of its blindness, from the darkness of evil. Being distorted, envy, fornication, inordinate affection, evil concupiscence and last but least covetousness. These are bits and pieces of, the traits, that Terra, has experience being in, the lineage of Ed Dart. So she loves filthy and darkness, to hide, from the goodness of the sun. Soon Terra would be in complete, creature form, around Sam. See Sam, was the first, to tell Terra how nice she looks, the time in, Dr. Letchell office. But she was there, to kill him at the time, alone with the staff, but that comment, he gave her, she was very cleaver, to go home with Sam, and finish, the job there. But his family, was a darn distraction. With her and Sheila not getting alone, and having sex, with the son, to destroying both father and son relationship.

All of this, was Terra's plans alone, with her father's instruction, to lured, the son, from the father, to get Sam alone, to harm him, or to kill him, like they already had in mind. How ironic is, it that getting Sam is, very difficult, then both ladies getting caught, by the cops? As Terra, and Dana, both checking on Benjamin's restraints, before leaving, to go, to the hospital, to kill and steal. But before, they can go, Terra is, trying on, a pink blouse, with a mini flannel skirt, with nurse shoes, if looks could killed, this will be it. That mini skirt, will have Dana, want to hurt a man over her. Because, for Terra's big butt and hips, makes, the skirt talks back, when a man is looking, he will be very satisfied at what they seeing. Just one rule, can't touch. "Dana! Are we ready, to go?" asked, Terra. "I believe, we are, you have, the tools, we need?" asked, Dana. "I think so." said, Terra. "Let's go and see, if we can get, this guy." said, Dana. As Benjamin, heard what was said, for him to come undone, to seek help, from the authority. Benjamin knows, that time is, running out, for both women to be capture or killed. They have chosen, their own demise. As leaving

Benjamin in, a dark shack tied up in all kinds of filth, while trying, to work his restraint's off, so he can get going, before, the women can return. Benjamin knows, if he can go to a nearby neighbor's house, to notify the authority he can save his brother-in-law, and get both of the dangerous women and put them back, where they belong. "All shuck's, my leg is, going to sleep on me." said, Benjamin. Terra put his restraints on so tight, that it's cutting off his blood flow, so when Benjamin, moves, the restraint's moves too. But there's one problem, after Ben comes undone, he needs, to figured, a way out, because, the women lock, the door from the outside, and there's only one window, he may try, to go through, if he can fit, Because, Benjamin isn't no small individual, with 5'6" stature and all 215lbs of muscles. But that not going, to stop him, from saving a life, and protecting one life. Benjamin thought, of hiding around, the shack on their returned, but if they don't have Sam, I can alarm, the authority, Benjamin's thought. As he, work, the restraint's, a loose, which he was damaging his ankles and wrists, for that leveraged, that he needed, to breakthrough, the ties. Benjamin's left leg is, gone, to sleep on him again, to keep him, from running or walking like he should. He broke all the ties, and now he is free, to get out of there, but the door, to the shack is lock, from the outside, so Benjamin, will need, to climb out of the window, that his niece, climb out, getting away, from Ed at the time of her being hostage. As Benjamin, looking around in, a dark shack, to found a way, to get out. He came, to the window, that Sheila had, to climb out, to make his getaway. Only one problem is, it's a small window and Ben is, a big man. He thought of yelling, for help, but that's no good, when you are in the middle of nowhere. Meanwhile both Terra and Dana, has arrived on hospital grounds, to go in, and get Sam. But they are in for a rude awakening, to know, that Sam's room is being guarded around, the clock. With Jon and Sheila, there in the waiting area, to see all that comes in and goes out. So the women, split up and came into, the hospital through different entrance doors, to carried out their plan still, to get what they want. As both women, starting on, the bottom floors, looking, for the man, on both ends of the hospital. Dana knows, that this one particular room, had a guard, at the door, and she thought, on the money, that's the room. But there is an armed guard there, so she goes, to meet Terra, on the other floor, to revised their plans. But Terra, has, another way of get him out of there. With her conniving ways, will use her cunning techniques on the guard. As Dana, met up with Terra, to let her know of the guard. To Terra, the guard isn't, a problem, for her, as she plays a nurse, in getting Sam out of his room. Terra, goes and get a wheelchair, to remove him, from the bed, into the wheelchair, to x-rays. "Hi I'm removing, him for a moment, to take him, for an x-ray." said, Terra. As the guard, let her by. While Dana, goes, to get the van started, Terra is getting help, from the guard, to put Sam into the wheelchair, so she could roll him, down to the van, to get going. With Sam, being heavy sedated, he didn't know, if he was coming or going. But Terra was confused, about which exitdoors, Dana told, her to report too. As fast, as Terra moving Sam in the wheelchair, could cause an accident, for moving like that. Finally, Dana, pulls in front of the exit, and Terra is making her way, with Sam relaxing. Just as she, make a run one security guard, asking where were they going, and Terra went over, to claw, the guy, and left out the doors, with Sam. As both women, took Sam, and lay him down in the cargo area of the van. And Dana peeled rubber, getting out of there.

Now Jon and Sheila, isn't aware, that their father is missing from his room, neither, the nurses. As one nurse, decides to check on Sam, and she asked, the security guard, "where is Mr. Bentford?" asked the nurse. "A nurse, came and took him to x-ray." said, the guard. "There aren't any x-rays, going on at this hour." said the nurse. "All f**k! Notify the cops!" said, the security guard. The nurse ran to the desk, to call the cops then she has to tell Sam's children, that their father is missing. It's not going, to be easy, telling Jon and Sheila, that their father was taken, from his room, by a couple of women. After the nurse, was done on the phone, she goes and approached Jon and Sheila, to explained, that their father was taken, somehow, and by who, they don't know. "Excuse me, I take it, that you both are Mr. Bentford's son and daughter, we are waiting on the authority, to arrive, your father is missing." said, the nurse. "What in the f**k are you talking about missing? Asked, Jon. "How did this happened, with security guard guarding, his room?" asked, Sheila. "Now what!?" asked, Jon.

"We are waiting on the law enforcement, to arrive." said, the nurse. As Jon walking back and forth, to think in who could want their father, and one someone, comes to mind, that is Terra McKenzie, of course. Now finding her is, the thing, as Jon thought. While Sheila is sitting and pouting, with cussing under her breath. Now as the cops arrived, to get a statement from the security guard, that was on the room, at the time, when Mr. Bentford was removed. The sergeant on the case is James Philpot who thinks, that hospital surveillance ought, to pick up anything and everything, that was done on hospital grounds. Now with everyone in the same room, to look and see what took place hours ago. As everyone, take a closer look, at the security monitors, and there is Terra dress as a nurse, and she is removing Mr. Bentford, with the help, of the same security guard, which he doesn't know, what is going on.

He thought he was helping, a real nurse. "That's Terra McKenzie." said, both Jon and Sheila. "Waited a minute, she is wanted, in the deaths of Dr. Letchell and his Staff." said, the sergeant. "And she is wanted, for other homicides, she committed." said, the sergeant. "Who is that, with her?" asked, the sergeant. "Hey that's the women, trying, to pick a fight, with my sister and I." said, Jon. "Her name is Dana Lynn." She is wanted also for murders she committed." said, the sergeant. So you telling us, that both women are in on our father disappearance?" asked, Jon. "I think, they had something, to do with our uncle disappearance too." said, Jon. "What's his name and when was he missing?" asked, the sergeant. "His name is Benjamin Tills." said, Jon. "We are still working, on his case, he's a former cop, from Hawaii?" asked, the sergeant. "He was missing all last month, from the post office." said, Jon. "And yes, he is still missing." said, Jon. "Well I have, a report, and it would be in amount of time, before we catch these women, stay clear of them, because, they are armed and dangerous." said, the sergeant. The minute, Jon heard that, in one ear, and out the other. Jon isn't, worried about some darn women, with weapons, all matter is, they have his father, and maybe his uncle, and he is, thinking dangerous himself. Now when it's your love ones like his father is in, a situation and very vulnerable, fragile may say, then the stakes, just went up. Because, your parent's life is at stake. Jon and Sheila have, lost their mother, to an insane lunatic, so now it's the father's turned. "Hell No!" Jon thought. So he takes, every avenue, to getting both his father and uncle back in one piece. Jon knows, it wants, be easy, to do, if bullets are, the source. In Jon's head, he thought that, this nightmare, was over, a year ago. But when evil keeps on charging at walls, to keep chaos in reign, Jon knows, also that he, can put, the nail in, the coffin, at any time sooner than later. Jon and Sheila, aren't taking thing, so lightly, with their father's failing health, so with his kidnapping, makes things much messy and worst. But gritty and nasty, for Jon to get both his father and uncle back unharmed and in peace, isn't a challenge, for Jon. But a war, for both sides. Now Jon has, to be very courageous in doing, the right thing, in looking, for a starting point, to find his family. He isn't listening, to a guy, a badge, with a gun, to tell him, what he already knows, and now, all Jon needs is an open window, to go in and do what needs, to be done. That is, to treat, both women like a fellow man, wanted, to be treated. Jon was raised, to treat women with respect, but these ladies are doing, a man's work, so he will try, to send both women, to their owned demise like a man. "An eye, for an eye, a tooth for a tooth." Jon thought. As Sheila knows, that Terra did, this. Because, when Jon shot Ed, and the creature, we hurt Terra bad, for killing her father, so now, a father, for a father." Sheila thought. "Jonny, this b**ch! better not harm, our father, and I meant that, I'm so ready, to knock, this b**ches head clean off her shoulders, for all this havoc, she and her b**ch ass partner, that looks like dude is doing." said, Sheila. "Hey sis! remember, when Ed removed you, from your room, a year ago?" asked, Jon. "Yeah, what of it?" asked,

Sheila. Then it just hit her like, a ton of bricks, there is a pattern, that one creates, for the seed, to pick up, where the one who created it leaves behind. So Terra is, doing what exactly, her father had started. She is doing everything that, her father has done The same parasite, that was in him, was passed on, to her. And once that parasite, grows evil and it's only knows, to kill.

With Sam's condition, he may not hold up, a lot longer, without being treated, for a mild heart attack, that left his arm, in a limp, and a slight drop in his jaw. As Terra and Dana, made it back, they notice, that the shack doesn't look like, the way it was left. The window, looks a little different in front of the place. While mumbling, to themselves, to where neither one wasn't understanding each other, with bewilder looks on, their faces, that someone messed up again. Because, Benjamin, has escape, and now Terra is really angry, with everybody, even Dana. Until they started, to arguing, with one another, about mistakes, so Dana had to tell, Terra about herself, that she herself, tied Benjamin's tie's, before leaving the place. "Look damn it! You are suppose, to have my back! So have my back, and do your damn job!" said, Terra. "I'm doing my Job, but your mistakes aren't my mistakes! So let's be very clear on this, stop trying, to put your problem on me! And owned up, to your mistakes!" dana, said. "Dana! Shut up! And stay out of my face!" said, Terra. At one point, the women had pulled, their piece on the other, and then act, as one going, to shoot, the other. But they dropped, their guns and started laughing, because, evil wouldn't unfolded on itself, they need each other. But the time, for evil, to live together, evil shall die together. Just like, that old saying, live by the gun, die by the gun. This is, what the ladies are intended, to do. They are going out, like a couple of bad to, the bone type of women, but only in, their minds. No evil house can't stand divided, they must work together, for in order things, to work accordingly. See these women, doesn't have men, to tell them what to do, Terra and Dana can do, without guys, but quick, to kill a guy, at the drop of a hat. So now, both of the ladies, would go and tried, to find Benjamin, and bring him back or execute Sam, if he doesn't return, to them.

But Benjamin isn't far, from the shack, he was waiting on, the ladies returned, to see if they had Sam with them. And they do have Sam with them. But Benjamin's left leg is, still in a limp situation, which cause, him, to dragged his one leg. But he is making noise, when he dragged his leg. Benjamin heard them pulled up in front of, the shack. As he tried, to keep quiet in the back of the shack. As he hears, the women arguing back and forth over mistakes and who's responsible. "These women, are insane, lunatic leads lunatic." Benjamin thought. So Benjamin, slowly walks over, to the biggest tree he spotted, to hide behind it, from the view of the women. Now Dana, goes, and looks around back of the shack, to see if Benjamin was hiding. But she sees, nothing, but if Terra comes out, to see, her sense of smell, would have found him behind, the tree. It was good, that Terra did, come out. Because, Benjamin, would have been executed on the spot, Now Terra and Dana, have thought, on moving again, because, their hideout has been compromised by a terrible mistake in bring Benjamin there, So they are looking, for the authorities, to show up next. So again, they need, another place, to lay low, and to figure out on, how to handle their hostage, Mr. Samuel Bentford. As they have Sam lying in a bunch of filth on the floor of, the shack. Sam is so weak, to put up a fight, so he just let whatsoever happen, happens. As Dana returns, from outside looking, for Benjamin in the back of the shack, but saw nothing. "So did you, see him out there?" asked, Terra. "No, not a thing insight." said, Dana. "We need, to find his ass, and bring him back here!" said, Terra. "Back here! Honey, we need, to move, this place is probably watch by now, and that moron, we had here been, going to show the cops, that we are here!!" said, Dana.

"Ok! you have a point!" said, Terra. As the temperatures drops into the teens, the shack is, the last place, to be, with Benjamin escape, it hard, to determined, if he went, to the cops, for help, or waiting to make a move on, the women. But for sure, he is trying, to help his brother-in-law, to stay alive. Suddenly, Benjamin picks up, a rock and threw it at, the roof of, the shack, to cause, a diversion, for Dana, to come out again, to see what was that noise, they heard. "What in hell is that noise?" asked, Dana. Her and Terra, just looked, at each other, to see who would go and check it out. This time, Terra came out, to look around, but she didn't come all the way, to the back, for Benjamin, to drop a huge branch, on the top of her head, to put her out, for a few minutes. As she headed, back around, to the front, to go back in. Now Benjamin needs, a better diversion, to come up with, to lured, both women out of the shack. As Sam, comes conscience, and looking around, in a dark place, wandering "what is this place?" as Dana and Terra, standing over him, with their weapons drawn on Sam. As the sunset, the evening is, far fetch, and the temperatures, are steady dropping, and the shack is freezing inside without a fire, to heat things up. So Terra, suggestion is, that Dana go, to find a couple of big logs, for a fire, while she keeps an eye on Sam. But if a fire, isn't started soon, everyone, would suffer, from hypothermia, except for Terra, being part women and part beast. But Sam and Dana would die from freezing. Now that, Jon and Sheila have arrived back home, "i can't believe, that b**ch snatched dad, from under beneath our noses, that burns me up!!" said, Sheila. "For the next, few days, we need, to be on our guard." said, Jon. "I hope, she brings her ass here! So I can get in it!" said, Sheila. "Now they have both dad and uncle Ben!" said, Jon. "So Jonny, what are we, going, to do?" asked, Sheila. "I'm thinking sis." said, Jon.

As Jon, thinking, for a better approach, to handle these particular women, like they wanted, to be treated. And with Sheila's involvement, she can handle Dana along, but not Terra and Dana both. See Sheila, wants Terra, for a long time coming, for messing, with her father. And starting mess between a father and son, then she tried, to kill Jon awhile back, to get and kill Sam later on. And Dana, Sheila wants her, for trying, to start mess in, the hospital, by staring and flipping her and Jon off.

Now that the temperatures have dropped tremendously, Ben knows, he needs to go back, to be with, his brother-in-law. Before, these women can do something evil, to him. So Ben is going back, to save his brother-in-law, from harm, if it's not too late. Therefore, Benjamin's heart is in, the right place, but at the wrong time. As he goes, back to the shack, to intervene in on their evil plans, to rescue Sam, but may be a risk coming back into, the situation. "Tap, tap and tap." A knocking at, the door. Both women just looked, at each other, with wide eyes, aiming at the door, with their weapons. "Hey! Ladies, it's me, Benjamin! it's cold out here, c'mon opened the door, it's just me." said, Benjamin. Dana slowly open, the door, with her piece, aimed at Benjamin's head, as she pulls him, through the door, by his shirt. "Man! You have some big ball's, to show your face back here! Who in the hell, are you to do that!?" said, Dana. "Hey I like being here, with you girls and by the way, I missed you too." said, Benjamin.

As Benjamin, stood there looking at Sam on, the floor, with a hospital gown on, freezing like's no one cares. As Benjamin offered, to go and get wood, to burn, to keep everyone warm. But Terra, had walked over, to Benjamin and hit him, with her gun on, the side of his face twice, to split him opened, until he started bleeding, from his temple. "That for leaving and coming back here, you old s.o.b!" said, Terra. Then Benjamin, held his head, then looks at Terra, like he wanted, to punch her dead in her face, for that little mishap. "So now, you can go and get some wood for us, but you better come back!" said, Terra. As Benjamin walks back out in, the cold to go and get logs of wood bleeding, from a lump on, the side of his head, makes him looks like he is going to pass out. But Benjamin knows, that he needs, some help by alarming the authorities there. If not soon, him and Sam are going, to die, in the hands of these insane women. Now as Benjamin drags a bunch of logs into the shack, he notices, that Sam is missing, with Terra as well. "Hey where's Mr. Bentford?" asked, Benjamin. "Oh! Don't you worry about him, he's none of your concerned! So put all that wood over here!" said, Dana. Now in the back of Benjamin's mind, there is, something, about to happen, to Sam, so he needs, to act quickly, to stop whatsoever is about to happen. As Dana makes, a retarded mistake, by sitting her piece down, to help Benjamin, with stacking wood and Benjamin notice she doesn't have her gun on her. So he did the unthinkable, by (Smack) Dana over her head, with a log, to put her out, for a while. "My Mom always told, me never, to hit a woman." said, Benjamin. "But oh well, sorry mom." said, Benjamin. Now as he quietly moves Dana out of sight, then he restraint's her and gag her mouth, to keep her quiet.

Benjamin grabs Dana's gun, to use it on Terra, if necessary. But saving Sam and his life is, what matter right now. Because, Terra is, extremely dangerous. And she is armed, so Benjamin has a right to shoot. Now as Benjamin walks slowly and quiet, to the other room, to see what is going on, as he is about to approaches, the door, to peek and see, Terra had her piece, at Sam's head unlocked and loaded. "Well c'mon in superman, and put the piece down now, or I'll blow a hole through his skull!" said, Terra. "And try me!" said, Terra. "I have my father's senses, and I heard, when you hit Dana on her head, so why did you, do that?" asked Terra. "I even heard when you ask about Sammy's whereabouts. "Now we are going out, to get Dana. Now Terra is about to go off on her protégé, to figured out how in the world, did this moron get her gun, Terra's thought. Now with both weapons, Terra goes, with Benjamin, to check on Dana, to see how bad she is hurting, for Benjamin's hit over, the head. "I'm thinking you gave her, a concussion, she isn't responding." said, Terra. Then Terra stood up, to put her gun, to Benjamin's face, to shoot him, for the trickery he just showed.

As Dana started, to come conscience, with her head hurting her, asking what had happened. But Terra was all over her, for laying her weapon down. And Terra turns, and looks, at Benjamin and shoot him in the foot (Pow!) "Ouch! Ouch!" said, Benjamin, hopping on one foot, then he fell to the floor. "I ought, to shoot you again, you piece of s**t! for what you have done!" said, Terra. "But I'm not going, to do that, I would like, for you, to watch me, to unload three rounds into Sammy boy." said, Terra. "Now how about that?" asked, Terra. "Now get your old ass up, and sit into this chair!" said Terra. As Benjamin stood up, on one leg, to sit down, with his shoe full of blood, and the bullet still in his foot. While Dana is, slowly getting up, off the floor, walking with Terra to the other room, where Sam is laying, to get his strength back. Now with a bullet in his foot, Benjamin is determined to save his brother-in-law life, if it cause him his life, so be it. So Terra came, and act quickly in, restraining Benjamin. To Terra, it didn't matter if he's bleeding, at the foot. She thinking he brought that upon himself, when he hit Dana on, the head. But Benjamin does have another plan, to get him and Sam out of there. See Dana or Terra's other guns are missing, from the suit case, where Terra keeps, all her and Dana's belongings. So Benjamin had taken them and hid them, to eliminated, their firing power. With this, can cripple, the women's way of fighting back. And eventually, they will run out of rounds sooner or later.

Now both women, are in the same space, talking among each other, about shooting Sam in, the head execution style, and then Benjamin, for being a witness, him as well. Then clear out and then start, all over elsewhere. But Dana is, trying to convince Terra, to do now, and leave. But Terra isn't really trying, at the moment, to hear, her protégé about leaving now. But Dana, do make a point in, leaving before everyone is on the verge of getting caught. But a person like Terra, will not listen, Because, she has it all figured out, on her own. She thinks in getting Sam and his brother-in-law, rub out and then go and getting Sheila and Jon also, then leave. But if she is thinking about getting Jon and Sheila, it's a chance and a challenge, for one, they can spot Terra coming at them, and two she makes a mess, before she gets there. But a challenge, yes, but no way in hell, she has a chance. The day, Terra, saw her father die, was the beginning of, her treachery and evil ways became, a normal thing. In which she vows, to revenge his death on those who are responsible, for his demise. So she and her protégé, decided, to capitalize on, this situation to fulfilled her revenge. And as the authorities, are starting, to comb, the area heavy with a national manhunt, for these two women. After the slaughter, both ladies, has left over at Nual's mansion and the killings of the father and his five sons, Dana's ex- boyfriend and the harlot killing, and Bobby Rauol and two more of Nual's men were found in, a field with the lady's DNA on the victims. Now how the authorities found out about Bobby Rauol, that Cain, has turned state evident, to get out on, a deal, if he talks. And he is, talking like a baby bird singing. For his time, to be short, so he can be with the woman, he fell in love with.

Now Sam's health is, deteriorating by the minutes, his breathing has become very shallow and looking blue in the face. But Terra and Dana are watching, this man die slowly, in their hands. "Like I said, A father, for a father." said, Terra. Standing over Sam's helpless body as death angels, waiting on a soul, to take. While Benjamin, in the other room, getting a loose again, to get Terra and Dana again, without being shot again. But his right foot is swollen, with the bullet still in it. As he tried's, to stand up on his right, it feels awful, to him, so going in there, to fight with these women, could put him, and Sam in harm's way. Benjamin could hear, Terra smacking Sam on the cheek. "That's for murdering, my father, you helpless bastard!!" said Terra. "I told, you that, I was going, to get you one way or another, So I brought, you here, to finish you off, then that piece of, s**t in the other room, we will do execution style on him, for messing everything up, then we are going, to get your precious Sheila and definitely Jon worthless ass." said, Terra. As all this was said, Benjamin has work himself loose, to get out the door, to hobble along, for help, But Terra, was a little too fast, for him to get up, the road to get help. Running on one leg is, impossible, to get to where you need, to get. As Benjamin hobbling along in, the road, Terra got close enough, to put one more round, into his arm, to bring Benjamin down. "Well why don't, I just kill you now and get it over with!" said, Terra. As she helps, Benjamin to his one good foot, and help him back, to the shack, to beat him, for running, from her.

Knowing Benjamin, never, never felt so humiliated in his life ever, until now.

Now as Sam lays on, the floor, verily breathing he raised his head, to see what is actually going on around him. But was too weak, to stand up, to fight. Not realizing, he is lying inside of a filthy shack, where his daughter was held hostage, a year ago. Now he's in the same situation, that Sheila was in, with Ed, but Sam doesn't know, that his brother-in-law is, in the other room, with a bullet in his arm, and one bullet in his foot. But he's alive and bleeding like crazy. Dana goes and check on her boss and girlfriend, to see if she needed her help. By the looks of things, that Terra has it all in control. "Hey how's he doing in there?" asked Terra. "He raised, his head, to see where he was at." said, Dana.

A Gangster's Help
Chapter X

Now weeks and another month gone by. And Jon and Sheila, hasn't heard anything on their father and uncle's whereabouts. But Jon shows, being skeptical, of the Sheriff department in trying, to locate both men. "Jonny, I had a dream, that Mom, and Dad we're gone on, a mini vacation, to Las Vegas, and on their way back here." said, Sheila. "Yeah, it would be nice for all us, to go on a vacation, when this thing blows over." said, Jon. "But first, we have to, get Dad and Uncle Benjamin back." said, Jon. "So again, Jonny what are we prepared, to do, for starters!" asking, Sheila. "Because, I'm ready, to do whatsoever it may take, to get Dad and Uncle Benjamin back here, where they belong." said, Sheila. As sitting at, the kitchen table, thinking how and which way, to go, for a start. But Jon, does, have some clues, to hit upon. "Hey Jonny! We need, to go to the store, to get a lot of things, that we are running low on." said, Sheila.

"Ok, so we can make it back, before someone decides, to call us." said, Jon. "Well it shouldn't take us, that long, I have a list of things we definitely need around here." said, Sheila. "Ok cool, you ready?" asked, Jon. "Yup!" said, Sheila. As every day, we as humans never know, how life can and will come at you. So we just take it or run with it. Funny and strange are, the words, that is, compared, to seeing something is, funny about this situation or this is, a strange thing, to take in. But no one seems, to be content, with life. They rather take funny, strange, then content. Because, content can scare, the very hairs off of your head, and it can. (A cop, gets behind you, and you don't have warrants, no citations, not even, a felony etc. Now he pulls you over, and question you about where are you going? then you speed off, because you aren't content, about what is about to happen.) But there isn't anything, to hide or to be afraid of, so we can be content. That's why most men and women alike run, from content, then just allowed content, to happen. Like a criminal, well there isn't much comparison, to stupidity. Most criminal's do wrong, and want you, to respect them, I think not. Like somebody, going into your bank account, so how can you, be content with that? Some people have extreme, self-temperance by controlling, their anger and keep being humble. What a way, to win things over. Right?

Let's take, the rise of society, against, the government, for instants. Just think, how strong, the people can come together and take back, the country, if they wanted too. For every politician, there is some corruption in his or her background. As people knows, but still allowed, that certain one into office. So it's not the politician fault, it's the system, the people are the system, because, a machine doesn't make choices, for people. Does a machine, tell a person, to chew and spit? So the rise of society can cause, the system, to default, by overthrow, the ones, that are in charge, and shown plenty of incompetence and incapable of getting and giving, the people what they need, and asking for. Before we get whatsoever, we need or asked for there's an argument between, the two incompetent parties, that they must point fingers, for not doing enough wrong, with just enough right, to be elected again.

Which would hurt, the most fearing God, the almighty? Or what a human can do, to you? Most would fear, the God of heaven and earth, because he is the one, that hand, the people over, to hell or call you home, and there isn't any stopping, to that. To where, another human can't do squad, but cause a lot of trouble, for him or herself. The most devious thing is, that some people know, that the system, may plot against them then others, but the others, do show love and respect, for the ones, that are plotted against. Gangsters are a modern-day Robin Hood of the community, they help those, that are in need, and can be very generous and modest at times. Some had thought, that the country, you love, could be ran by gangster's overnight. Why? Because, of the devastating and devious turns, that the leadership was going. People knows, that gangsters are not, to be played with. Dangerous and devious equal to killing, when going against, the grain. Nual is still looking, for revenge on, the women, who shot him and stole from him also. Now the man has, went throughout, the city, from east to west, north and south, looking for these two individuals, for some retribution and wacked, both ladies in a confrontation if can. As Nual, comes up short on his last cigarette, to tells his driver, to stop at the nearest market, for a pack of cigarettes, and tells his driver, to go in and get the cigarettes, while he sat, until his returned. Lord and behold, Jon and Sheila have pulled, into the markets parking lot, to find a place to parked. Usually Jon always tried, to get near the exit doors, for an easy in and out. Because, of Sheila wouldn't have to travel far, with all the groceries. Jon let's his sister out in front of the market, and then goes, to parked. How is, this so, he parks next, to Nual's limo. But Nual's driver, looks and just stares, at Jon like he some kind of insect. "Hey you, looks like you having a staring problem!" asked, Nual's driver. "You! The one has, a damn problem, you know, me? I don't think you know me!" said, Jon. "But if you, keep on staring at me, you will get a piece of this whooping." said, Nual's driver. "Look here! muthaf***er! Shut your hole up, and stop talking to me!" said, Jon. Quietly Nual, was in the back enjoying, both men go at it. Then he steps out, to intervene, before it turns physical between both men.

Jon was shock, to see Nual, getting out of this nice limo and now Jon and Nual starts, with each other. "Look dude, I'm here, with my sister, to shop and go home, we aren't here, to cause problems, so now what!?" asked, Jon. "Hey my man, take it easy man. I understand, where you are coming from, and I just wanted some info on those women, I being looking for." said, Nual. "I just wanted to know, if you or your sister seen them?" asked, Nual. "No! Those b**ches, has my father and uncle, and when I do find them, I will split both of their heads completely opened." said, Jon. "Hey look, I would love, to get in on that, these women shot me, and stolen, from me as well, so how about it, we come, together, and get these b**ches, and give them what they deserve." said, Nual. "Ok let's do that, we can meet, and goes over the particulars, and I let my sister know, about this talk, we had." said, Jon. "You do that man, so we can get this done, you just don't know, how much, I want both of those women." said, Nual. "That makes two of us, for damn sure." said, Jon. "Oh by the way, have you or your sister seen Cain?" asked, Nual. "The way, I took it, he is doing, his time, at the Lajunta correctional institution." said, Jon. "Well at least, he is safe, from all this chaotic bulls**t." said, Nual. "Yeah, he turned himself in, to the law, he told, my sister, that he got tired of running, from them, so he stopped running and joined them." said, Jon. As Jon and Nual, both standing there chuckling among themselves. "So, they have your father and uncle, you say?" asked, Nual. "Yup!" said, Jon. "And these same women shot you and stole from you too?" asked, Jon. "Oh Yeah." said, Nual. "They will reap what sow, I guarantee, you that." said, Jon. "Hey let's meet, at T&R Beer House on, the corner of Eugenio and Bess Road." said, Nual. "That not far, from us." said, Jon. "I'll see you there, let's say tomorrow?" asked Nual. "Tomorrow it is." said, Jon. As Nual, heads back to his limo, to leave, here comes Sheila, out of the market, with groceries', looking like she, saw a ghost. "Is that, who I think it was?" asked, Sheila. "I'll explain it, once we get home." said, Jon. "What he's looking, for Cain?" asked, Sheila. "No! I said, I'll explained it when we get back, to the house." said, Jon. Now Sheila's mind is, going back and forth, because, she is so curious, about her brother and Nual, conversing, with each other. As she just stared, at her brother while he is driving. "Jonny, can you tell me, a little bit, what you and him had discussed?" asked, Sheila. "Ok, since, you can't wait, he is joining up, with us, to find dad and uncle Benjamin." said, Jon. "What!!?" asked, Sheila. "Wait, a minute, I'm a little confused here, why is he joining us, for real?" asked, Sheila. "Those same two, tried, to kill him, and they both rob him also." said, Jon. "So he told, you that, and we suppose, to believe him?" asked, Sheila.

"Look sis, we need, all the help into finding dad and uncle Benjamin, and I think, this guy is, very serious on catching these morons, and putting a bullet in their heads." said, Jon. "So if you, don't wanna work, with this guy, stay home." said, Jon. "Jonny! How can you, say that to me, knowing, where dad and uncle Benjamin, means a lot, to me, and catching those b**ches and giving them hell is, all I wanted, to do." said, Sheila. "So take it back." said, Sheila. "Ok, sorry, for saying that, but we will meet, with him, tomorrow, at T&R Beer House, to discuss, the plans on get dad and uncle Benjamin back, before we kill those two." said, Jon. "What of the cops, get involved?" asked, Sheila. "Hell with the authorities, for as we are concerned, they not doing their jobs anyway." said, Jon. "Who ended Ed's life? I can have recalled, that I did, and cops showed up, when everything was done and handle, then they bring their punk asses in, to tried, to do somethings." said, Jon. "They talking, about building a case, for a trial, how in the hell, they are trying to build, a case, they need, to work on building two coffins', that's what they need, to do." said, Jon. "Jonny, please don't get, all work up, over this crap." said, Sheila. "I'm not, I just get so, agitated when you know, that certain things, need, to be put in check, but not." said, Jon. "Well my brother, somethings are out of our control, like we didn't know, that those heifer's, was going to grab dad, and Uncle Benjamin from beneath our noses." said, Sheila. "But it happened. And now we are sitting twiddling our thumbs like, the idiot's we are, for letting it happened." said, Jon. "Jonny! What are you, talking about, let what happened?" asked Sheila. "Really! You need, to listen, to yourself man." said, Sheila. "I'm really, starting, to think, that we let those evil women, just come in and do whatsoever." said, Jon. "But not our fault period, that all I have to say." said, Sheila.

As coming back, from the store, the house seems dark inside, Sheila neither Jon turned on any lights. But for safety, Jon enter in first, with his piece cock and loaded, to shoot if move and frightening him or Sheila. "Well, all clear" said Jon. Now him and Sheila can start bring in, the groceries', with the kitchen still in remodeling stages. That's before Ed's creature came in, to tear, the house apart, when no one was home. But they are putting the pieces back together slowly and sure this time. Afterwards putting up, the groceries', Sheila asked, Jon, to be careful, for tomorrow meeting up with, a bad person like Nual and his henchmen's. "You not going?" asked, Jon. "i thought, I wasn't going, with you." said, Sheila. "No, you can absolutely come, to help with some of the particular's on getting dad and uncle Benjamin back." said, Jon.

The minute Jon stopped talking, that's when, both Jon and Sheila heard something on, the front porch. It was, a deputy from the Sheriff department come, to get more information on the incident, that happen at the hospital. It happened so fast, no one knew, how the women came in and took Sam without being seen. But Terra and Dana, does have crucial and dangerous ways, on getting to their victims, they don't care for. The ladies, are good, at what they do, and they love the thought of killing, until they need, to indulge one another by preying on men especially. Jon looks, at Sheila and said, "Hey don't mention, a word about tomorrow." said, Jon. "And I already know, man." said, Sheila. As Jon opens, the door, to let the deputy in, to hear what he has to say. "Hi Mr. Bentford, I need, a couple of questions from you and your sister, if you don't mind." said, the deputy. "Did you both, ever see Terra McKenzie on the site?" asked, the deputy. "No. we didn't see her, all we seen was, the other girl, because, she flips us off." said, Jon. "And she, was trying, to pick a fight, with my sister." said, Jon. "It was ridiculous, for what she was trying, to do." said, Sheila. "We are still, mourning our mother, and now we don't know, our father health situation got any worst, as we speak." said, Sheila. "What get us is, how did they grab our father, without us seeing them is what I don't get." said Jon. "Well one was a distraction, why the other is at work." said, the deputy. "Well both women are very very clever and seems, to be also intelligent, that I may add." said, Jon. "And Terra, once stay with us, for a minute." said, Jon.

"We are within, forty-eight hours, to catching both women to preserved life, but the F.B.I is, involved, as well, for wanted dead or alive." said, The Deputy. "So for being, at large as long as they have, the Federal Bureau of Investigation is, now, a player in the manhunt." said, The Deputy. "And the U.S Marshall are playing as well." said, The Deputy. "So please bare, with us in catching these individuals, we are moving quickly on bring them in." said, The Deputy. "Well that's great news, for us to hear." said, Jon. But in Jon's, mind he hopes, that the law reaches them, before him and Nual could get to both women, and destroyed. Sheila, looks at Jon, to see what his response be, to the deputy news, but still, some determination in Jon's reactions. As once was, with Ed, being alive, how Sam and Jon's hearts was hardened, to the law, and take matters, into their own hands. In striking, a blow to the creature and Ed, into stopping the havoc, that cause, them, the town, and the victim's families.

As The Deputy was leaving, the Bentford's, Terra and Dana has decided, to take a closer look, to see what was happening, with the Bentford's home, to see why, the authorities, are there. Now both Sam and Benjamin, are alive, but not well. Now Sam is still holding on, by a thread, and Benjamin's foot starting, to see gangrene due, to blockage and not enough blood flow. Both men need, some medical attention soon or both can die in the hands of women. Now the room, that Sam is in, has become quite quiet, and no one is standing over him, he is trying to strengthen himself, to get out of there. Now Sam isn't aware, that his brother-in-law is in, the other room, with a bullet in his shoulder and one bullet in his foot. As Sam makes his way, to the doorway of the room, he sees, his brother-in-law, sitting there in pain. Sam asked, Benjamin "Hey Ben, you ok, where are we?" ask, Sam. "I don't know, but we got to, get out of here, soon." said, Benjamin. With the sun shining, Sam could tell, that they are near the house, but Benjamin, didn't know that, because of him coming back, to the area, and need, to know where everything is. "Where are both of those heifers at?" asked, Sam. "They both, went outside, to look at something." said, Benjamin. For Sam, not to be in good health, he stood up, to see were both women we're at. "OMG! They are spying on, the house, I can see my backyard, from here." said, Sam. "What! You telling me, that the house is, twenty second away to your backyard, I didn't, exactly know, where I was at." said, Benjamin. "Hey Ben, you being gone, for how many years?" asked, Sam. "Hey never mind, that Sam, we need, to get out of here, so come and help me up would you?" asked Benjamin. "Ben I can't lift your big ass up, all you are going, to do is bring me to where, you are." said, Sam. As both men chuckle. "Well we aren't in, the best of shape, to fight, with these broads, which I do know, that both of them can beat our asses, to a pulp, so just sit still Ben." said, Sam. "Oh here, they come." said, Sam. As Sam, goes back into, the room and Benjamin sat still, the women both came in, from outside, as they both stared at, Benjamin, then, they just chuckle at one another. They both were very indulge, at the progress, they had created. And not knowing, that there is, bigger problems and trouble, ahead for both women. As the authorities, Gangster, and family members are looking for, both women. But not good, for all government agencies, to come on board to correct things and make things back normal. Now Jon, has a made up mind, to team up, with Nual after all, to get these women and shut them down, quick and for good. By now Sheila is, thinking of not getting involved, and let Jon and Nual does, what needed, to be done. But also her father is, on her mind, for her to have, a play into the ordeal. "I just wanna ring, the life out of these evil b**ches!" said, Sheila. "Why does, Terra acts like her darn daddy?" asked, Sheila. "she has, her father's traits, that why she is doing what she is doing." said, Jon. "Believe it, Ed was, a lot worst, then her but was ever, to be he shows up, a beast, then, a damn man, to pretend, to be dad's friend, after he killed mom, s**t!" said, Jon. With a lot of anger in his voice. "I'm just glad, that s.o.b is dead, and now we have to put his daughter in the dirt, with him." said, Jon. "One thing, I can't get over is, that I had sex, with that evil b**ch, then she calls, herself coming between dad and I, what a bomber." said, Jon. "Jonny, your nasty, I can't believe, you had sex, with that b**ch, I'm so disappointed in you, for doing that, all the girls, that's here in Lajunta, you needed, to mess with her!?" asked, Sheila. "Well my sister, I was a desperate man, with a little horniest, which I haven't held, a woman in a while." said, Jon. "But she did open my eyes, boy, it felt good, to be able, to have great sex again or be next, to a girl." said, Jon. "Shuck's she had, more, then just your eyes opened nasty!" said, Sheila. "But now, we have to kill, that whore, before she turns, into a monster, like her darn daddy did." said, Jon. "i couldn't believe he was, the creature all this time, and had us fooled wow." said, Sheila. "All that I know, is that dad and uncle Benjamin, better be alright, that's all I have to say." said, Sheila. "Well they both, are very strong men at heart, but physically they are weak older men." said, Jon. "And all, I have to say, is they both better live." said, Jon. "I had a dream, that I sat Terra on fire, and let her butt burned too." said, Jon. "That's a very nice, and diabolical thing, to do." said, Sheila, with a chuckle. "I said, that I had, a dream, that I sat her on fire, I don't wanna do that, because we will, come to her level of, things." said, Jon. "Excuse me! Have you forgot, that her father killed our mother, or let see, where is dad and uncle Benjamin? That's right, they aren't here! so what is the freakin difference man! if you do or not?" ask, Sheila. "So your point is?" asked Jon. "Burn her! That's my point, a f**kin murder, doesn't deserve any recognition, so do you understand me now?" asked Sheila. "That can be arranged, by you alone." said, Jon. "Me?" asked Sheila. "Yes you, so now, don't get all timid on me now, you spoke of it, why don't you make it happened?" asked, Jon.

Now we can understand, certain people like, to see things done, but asking, them to do it. Can be a problem, because, he or she is the very same person say and speak on it, but makes not one effort, into helping put things into motion. Just like Sheila likes, to see Terra burned, for real. But not, the one to do it. Passing, the buck is, the true words, to look for. But Sheila has, a point in destroying, a half person, half beast of, a gal, that has her father's traits, can't be trusted, for good. Terra is, all about the evil of it. Nevertheless, to say, that others, are at stake. With revenge served, as a dish cold. But can good, prevail, and rise, to the occasion? As time running out and against Terra and her accomplice, with law enforcement on their trails heavy indeed. And with the following day as Jon meets up, with Nual and two of his henchmen's, trying to nail, the women, before the law enforcement can get to them, to save, that needs, to be destroyed. But as Jon thinking, how can you save something, that doesn't want to be save? Jon's thought. So can you reason with it? There isn't, a way to reason, with evil. The Bible has taught us, that you can't be friends with an evil being, because, some time or another they will turn on you, for speaking, about doing good, or saying great things about another or most of all, keeping on a positive note. Now that would likely, get you killed, by the likes of Dana and Terra. Only in her sanctuary, you will commit, a way of life upside down, and work it left, instead of right, positive stance on anything, may be, a one-way ticket, to be next to her father's god, which is Satan himself. Now if, that sounds, like an interesting living, they need you for their military of wickness. Be not deceived: evil communications corrupt good manners. 1Cor 15:33. Now as Nual speaks on looking at all abandon home and shops, "because, they have a tendency, to hide in abandon places. This way for them, to stayed out of the spot light." said, Nual. "Well we have abandon home, all over the place." said, Jon. "There is, a shack, that's on the other side of the tracks, where my sister, was held hostage, we can check there first. "said, Jon. "Ok, let's do this, and get these b**ches!" said, Nual. "And I will be glad, when this is completely over, I'm so tired of, cleaning up before, the cop can do, a thing." said, Jon. "Well Jon, it's an honor, to work with, a future cop." said, Nual. "Ha ha yeah right." said, Jon. "Hey no mercy, for these whores, that I do mean that." said Nual. "I'm totally with you on that man." said, Jon. "See I wouldn't, careless about, these freakin evil women, until, that one shot me in, the shoulder, then the other one took my money, and both of them split, trying, to leave me, for dead, well they f**k up! Big time." said, Nual. "So now, it's my turned, to make, a powerful statement not to f**k me over ever." said, Nual.

Now as the guys, get into motion, to do their own way of justice, to take matters, into their own hands, could be very and quite dangerous, but what's a couple of women, to them? Incompetent, don't know, which way is down and going sideways and not backwards. But over time, both women have grown, into knowledge, about the streets, and being fugitives. But wisdom on having weapons of destruction is, where both do lack in. Now Dana, being the oldest out of the two, does, have shooting experience, from her pass years of murdering several victims. But Terra, on the other hand, has some whip, about killing, after she murdered, her coworkers and boss, at a medical clinic, to helping her father, to carry out, a vicious vendetta, against a family, that is harmless. By under estimating, these two killers, as women, could shut Nual and Jon down if ever confronted. No man stands firmly, with these women, and make it another day. As Nual and Jon pulls closer, to that shack, where Sheila was, held hostage, to see, if anyone was inside. As both men started, walking towards, the rundown shack, but not, a sound, but the door, was open, and dark inside, "You have a flashlight, in your vehicle, so we can see?" asked, Nual. "Yup let me get that, quickly." said, Jon. Now both men are inside of the messy and rundown shack, to find clues and evident, that someone was there.

"Hey look at this, it seems, to me that someone has being shot cause, there's blood all over here on the floor." said, Jon. "I think, this is fresh blood, it's mighty obvious, that they hide here, because, the way this place looks, no one would have suspected, that there was anyone here." said, Nual. "Now freakin, what!?" asked, Jon. "We are going, to continue, to look, until we catch up, with them, so are you with me?" asked Nual. "I told, you, that I want these b**ches, as well as you do too." said, Jon. Now Terra and Dana, must have sense, that someone or somebody, was coming, to the spot, because, they have clear out, before being caught, but luck was on the girl's side. They just didn't know, that Nual and Jon, was that close on catching their butts in a nick time. But they want be as lucky next time. "Now where could they be?" asked, Jon. Not knowing, that the ladies has, a weird twisted of, humor, that isn't very delighted, that is move more close, to home. Now that Nual and Jon, will take, a five-mile radius, a day in trying to help consume, the women's whereabouts. Terra and Dana, are on their way, to Sha'vore county, with Benjamin and Sam tied helpless in the back of, the van. But to find somewhere else, to lay low, for a descent minute. But out of, the law enforcement way. But they have, one tricks up their sleeves, that no one thought, they would do. Now the women have disguises, to mislead, the public and the community. With Benjamin and Sam on, their sides facing one another and whispering about yelling, for help, but might get them both shot, for a stupid move. "I'm wondering, where in the f**k are they taking us?" asked, Benjamin. As Sam, trying, to gasp, for air. "Sam! Sam!" Hey he gasping, for air!" said, Benjamin.

"Stopped! And check, and see, hats up with him." said, Terra. As Terra hold, the weapons on them, so no one can get a crazy ideal, and trying, to run or yelled. "His breathing is very shallow, we are about, to lose him." said, Dana. "I do know, that he has heart issues, for real." said, Terra. "We're not taking him back, to the hospital**k that!" said, Terra. "And the way, I look, at it, again, a father, for a father." said Terra. Benjamin just stares, the heck at her, for saying, stuff, like that. But he knows, in his mind, that he needs, to do something quick, or he is going to lose, his brother-in-law forever.

As sitting on, the side of the narrow road next, to a farmland Terra is, getting, a wicked ideal of, dumping Sam off on, the side of the road, for dead. But Dana, has another planned in mind. Now some of, the money, that they had stolen, from Nual, well Dana had, suggested, that, a hotel, for a day, would be, to lay low, would be good. "You must be losing, your damn mind, for us, to be trap in, a hotel!" said, Terra.

"Ok! Do you have, a better ideal, since everything, you think of, has failed?" asked, Dana. "Look b**ch! Don't start, with me, I'm already under a lot of pressure, trying, to keep us, from getting caught, with law enforcement on our asses, so you aren't making things easy." said, Terra. "Ok, I'm so sorry, sweetie." said, Dana.

As Sam and Benjamin, thought that everything, was about, to unfold in their presence. But both women knew, each other quite well, but both women know, that they need each, to live another day, but both ladies, final destination isn't quite ready yet. But soon will arrive in, an unusual way, but least unexpected. "So sweetie, what do you recommend, for us to do?" asked, Dana. "Now this may sound, a little far fetch, but this may work, so be with me, on this please?" asked, Terra. "Hon, I'm always, going to be, with you, matter what, I will die, with you, that's why I love you Tee." said, Dana. "My feelings for you are as mutual, as it gets." said, Terra.

Now with warm weather coming, to warm things up, can be, a relief, for things, to be much better, to find and get around without being miserable, and frustrated in the cold temperatures. But Dana is, waiting, to see what Terra's planning, to do, with both Benjamin and Sam, because, Dana knows, that every plot, that Terra has put in play, has fail miserably, and a shame, to tell her, what she already knows, but doesn't want to hear it, like she told, her so, which Dana is right, but want say, a word. Dana is, afraid, that she corrects Terra's mistakes could also put her in, the hot seat, to be rid of. So Dana would just turn and look, the other way, to kiss up, to her girlfriend and protégé, for peace, or speak kind, but bold, not in, a harmful way, that her mess ups, are causing various havoc on each other. So as Terra is, driving like a bat straight into hell, she seems, a bit nerves, because, her hair is starting, to grow, a bit longer, then usual, and her nails looks like talons of, a bird. As she starts, to transformed in, a way, that Dana never seen before.

"Ok, Tee, you better slow down, before we wreck." said, Dana. "I got it." said, Terra. As she headed back in, the direction they came. But to county route road. Now that's Sam's road, to his home. As both men lying helpless on, their sides facing one another wandering what in, the hell, are these women are up too. But not knowing, that Terra is, about to strike at home, like she had planned all alone. Now Sheila is, there by herself, waiting on Jon, to get back. But Jon and Nual are on, a heavy goose chase into another area, to where they think, that Terra and company would be. But only, be disappointed, that they want be there. So the men are looking into various areas and not the places, that should be looked into. And again, these women are so clever, and intelligence can speak, for itself. And evil is, having it way, for a season, with patience running out, for the upright, but not giving up on exterminating evil, for once, and for all. But too bad, that one's lives must be sacrificial and, the others are carried, to safety, for preserving.

Tee's Plots Failed

Chapter XI

Now as days, are longer, and the weather seems, to be, a blessing, for some. Cain is in great spirits, to know, that he is out on excellent behavior. As he is escorted, throughout, the county correctional facility. And all he can think of is, Sheila's face. But he may have to, do some explaining on being Terra's accomplice, because of Nual's information he gave her month's prior. But that's not going, to stop progress in, their friendship on to, a relationship of course. Now that Cain is out, he needs a ride, to see his favor lady. But needs a way there. So he does, the old fashion way, Cain hitch hike, to be a surprised, to Sheila. Now as Terra pulls, the van several yards, from Sam house, down the road next, to a farmland and the ideal is, to walk up the road, to the house, with Sam and Benjamin and everyone in one spot, for a deadly execution style. This is, all for her daddy's sake. As Terra uses, Dana, to get Sheila, to the door, to come out, and to help both her father and uncle, for them, to barge, their way into, the house and take charge over them all.

Once inside, the house, Terra drops Sam's body and attack Sheila right away, by hitting her on, the side of her head, for retribution, from the last time, as Terra watch her father die at the hands of, Jon. "That's pay back, you b**ch!!" said, Terra. While Dana, wanted, a piece of Sheila as well. "This one is, from, the hospital, you whore!" said, Dana. As she slaps Sheila hard across, the face, while her father lying, with very little breath in his body, and her uncle sit helpless, watching, Sheila be pound on, by the other women. But Sheila, isn't a push over, when it's time, for her to defend herself. As she fights back, with both women, but Dana and Terra both wasn't letting up. While one sat on top of Sheila, and the other one holds Sheila down, to keep her, from defending herself. As female's are, they don't fight fair, when a two on one and calling it fair, with equal. Now Cain has arrived, at the Bentford's, but something is well wrong, because seeing, that van down, the road on, the other side next to, the farmland is, the van, that he left, the women with. As he approaches, the porch, there was yelling and fighting inside. "Terra and Dana, all s**t." Cain thought. Now Cain knows, he needs, to intervene somehow some way but quick. "I'm so tired of these two b**ches, I know what I need, to do." as Cain thinking, to himself. "if I can, draw one or maybe both outside, this would give Sheila, a break." Cain, thought. As Cain goes, to the front window, to glance in, to see actually, what's going on. Cain sees Terra wailing on Sheila, while Dana holding Sheila legs, so she can't fight back. "All s**t, they are attacking my girl, and both are going, to pay for that dearly." Cain, thought. While being very quiet around, the house, Cain needs, a distraction, to throw, the women off beat, to come outside. But if he can get Dana, to come then Terra is really worthless, without Dana.

So Cain's ideal, was to throw, a rock through, the window, and run up, into the barn, to have Dana or Terra, to come out after him. And Cain is, looking, for a nice size rock, to throw at the window, for a distraction. (crash) as, the glass shatter in the kitchen floor. "What in the hell, was that!?asked, one of the women. As Cain peeks, out at the back of the house, both women are trying their best, to figure out, what just happen. Looking at each other, with bewilder looks, and confused as hell. Suddenly the back door opens, and it's no other, then Dana, to check things out, while Terra's big butt stays inside. As Dana steps, down off of the porch, to go around, the house, to see who is there. But she saw no one, so she walks back, the way she came, then she heads, to the barn, to see if anyone, was there also. Now as she, comes deep into the barn, there we're sacks of seeds, for Sam's garden, that he keeps up in the top loft of the barn. As Dana, trying her best to shoot, whatever moves. Cain was waiting, for perfect timing, to let, the rope go, for his target, to be on point. Cain dropped, two bags of seeds, on Dana head, to put her out, for the law enforcement, to get her.

As he gets down, to tied Dana up, and gag her mouth, to keep her from, screaming for help, now it's Terra's turned, for her to get some of Dana's situation. "I finally, get your sweet looking ass, too." said, Cain. While tying up Dana, as she, lying unconscious. But he carried her into, a dark corner of the barn, so she can't be seen, by Terra. Now Terra comes out yelling, for Dana "Dana! Dana!! what in the f**k is going on here!?" Terra asking herself that. "Dana! Where are you!?" asking, Terra. Cain stood, to where he can see Terra on the porch, looking stupid as could be. But inside, Sheila has gotten up, off of the floor, with a bloody nose and one of her eyes are blacken, from Terra's punches. But Sheila, doesn't know, that Cain is there, helping them. As she goes and check on Sam, but no responds out of him. Sheila checks, for a pulse and there wasn't a pulse. "daddy! daddy!! daddy!!!"as she cried while calling him. Sam was dead, when he hit the floor, and still lying into. The same position. "Oh my God!! oh no!" said, Sheila. As she cried into, her father chest, while Benjamin sat against, the wall, thinking he was trying his best, to do something, to keep Sam out of harm's way. But he, to fail him as well. Benjamin's thought.

As it getting late, Jon and Nual, are headed back, and tried tomorrow. "It's getting late, and I need, to check on my sister to see if any news, about my father and uncle." said, Jon. "Hey man, I definitely, understand, so tomorrow, we say, the same time?" asked, Nual. "Hey can you follow me home, I have something, to show you, if you don't mind?" asked, Jon. "I'm ready." said, Nual. Now when Jon, hit his home, he would sense, something is wrong. But he is willing, to make it right. Terra's is on her own, since she doesn't know, where in the hell is, Dana. But everyone knows, that Terra is every bit of her father, that means, she is going, to end up like her father and die like him as well. Now Sheila is in a rage, because her father shouldn't die like he did.

So Sheila, went back, to her father's bedroom, to grab both his glock 34 and his mossburg double barrel shotgun. She came and gave the shotgun, to her uncle, and she kept, the glock 34. And as she waited, for Terra's returned, for her and uncle Benjamin to blast Terra ass, to hell. But Terra is, standing between, the house and the barn, looking to see where is Dana. Terra is looking at the shack, to see if Dana, went back, for something. But no way, she doesn't want no part of the barn, as she starts, to walk back inside of, the house, with death waiting on her. Sheila is, getting into, a good position, for to blow Terra's head off, just like her brother Jon did, Terra's dad.

As Terra coming into, the house, she stood there looking, to see, where did Sheila go, so she can finish beating her up. But Benjamin, had a drop on her, when she came, to the livingroom, and right away Sheila shoots, Terra twice (Pow! Pow!) and Benjamin place one in her chest area (Boom!). Terra fail, to the floor, with orange like plasma running out of her, As Sheila, falls, to floor, leaning on her father breathless body, crying emotional. Then minutes later, Cain comes running into, the house, to see what happen. Because, he heard gun shots fired. But he walks over, to Sheila, and hugs her, but she looks, to see who was hugging on her and she was very shock, to see Cain. "Hey honey it's me." said, Cain. As Cain looks, down on both dead bodies of Mr. Bentford and Terra's. As Jon drives up, into the driveway, he noticed, that there are more people in the house besides his sister. Jon walks in, and see Sheila and Cain, standing next, to his dad thinking something wrong with dad. Jon realized, that his father is gone. "So what in God's green earth happened here?" asked Jon. "Well I hitch hike, to get here, and when I arrived, I heard, a lot of commotion going on inside, so I kept quiet, so I can see what was going on, both women were pounding on your sister, so I'm sorry for breaking, the glass out of the back window there, I had to make, a distraction, to get them both off of Sheila." said Cain. "Wait, where is the other evil women?" asked Jon. "Well I gag her and tied her down, in the barn, for the law to get her, when they get here." said, Cain. "So Cain, you did a helluv job, in protecting my sister, we need, people like you, to help in every way." said, Jon.

"Well let me called, the authorities, so we can move on." said, Jon. As stands over his old man body, trying to hold back tears, as he sat next, to his sister. "Cain, can you, tell Nual, to come in, for a moment?" asked, Jon. "Nual, outside?" asked, Cain. "yeah." said, Jon. Now that both Nual and Cain has returned inside, they both come in arguing, about the whereabouts of Terra and Dana. "Guy's! Please! we don't need, to go any further, my sister and uncle got this evil b**ch." said, Jon. "Wait a damn minute! Where is the other b**ch at?" asked, Nual. "Nual come, with me!" said, Cain. As they both, with Jon as well, walks out, to the barn, to get Dana, and bring her inside, for the authorities, to pick up. All three guys went out and she was still unconscious, gaged and tied up. Cain, lifted her up and over his shoulder, she goes. Benjamin needs to go to the hospital, to remove a couple of bullets, while everyone was waiting on the authorities, to get there to remove Dana and the coroner office, to come and remove Sam and Terra's corpses. While waiting, for the authorities, Nual despitefully kick's Terra's dead lifeless corpse "Her ass is, very lucky, because, I still, wants, to put one in her, you b**-ch!" said, Nual. "Well man, she is gone, this place is better off without her." said Cain. As Dana, coming conscience, trying to wander, what is going on, why is she, tied up and gagged. But she was looking down at her dead and lovable boss and girlfriend, it's hard to believe, that her Terra is gone. Nual walks over and pulls his piece out and put it at the head of Dana "it's not, too late, for you to joined your buddy, over there with her, your worthless piece of s**t!" said, Nual. "This b**ch, stole my money, from me, and that dead b**ch there, shot me in my shoulder, so let's join her in spirit!" said, Nual. "Nual! C'mon man, please put your gun, away don't go, to prison, for killing, this evil crap of a person." said, Benjamin. "Hey Nual, my uncle is, absolutely right, man you have your freedom, but if you shoot her, she dies also, while you are sitting in prison, but no one wins this one, so don't do it man." said, Jon.

As Nual listening, to the retired cop, that spoke plenty of knowledge, to a violent individual like Nual, who accepts to listening, to a wise person. But can't say, the same, for trouble women, like Dana and Terra. Dana will be fully prosecuted for, the crimes she committed. And the Judge will determine, her fate, by sentencing her, to death, by execution. So after all she may see Terra again in death. "I'll be seeing you around, let me get out of here, before the cops get here, I hate copes, and cops don't like me." said, Nual. "Nual, thanks again for helping me out." said Jon. As Cain and Sheila walks out on, the front porch hand in hand, talking about moving, to Ohio, to get out of Lajunta, because, of the fond memory of her mother and now her father is lingering always. "Now this house has, becomes, a tomb, to me, for me and Jonny, with all that happens here can stay here, but I do want, to move." said, Sheila. But Cain, understood her and the message, she is expressing. "Sheila, will you marry me?" asked, Cain. "Oh course, yes! I will marry you." said, Sheila.

Cain grabs, Sheila and hugs her, like never before. "Oh honey, this feels so good, to know, that I have, a great, woman that loves me back, and Sheila, sweetie, I will never, leave your side, as long as I live, I promised, for darn sure." said Cain. "I will, always hold, you to that mister." said, Sheila. Now Sheila couldn't be as happy, for her father, just passed away, as she watches, the coroner officers, takes her dad's corpse away in, the van, which is very sad, to see, the one you love, so much is gone on, to glory, but never forgotten.

Benjamin comes and embrace her and Cain. While they make room, for Terra's corpse as well. Without immediate family, Terra's corpse, will be cremated, and her ashes, will be dump on the South Platte or near, the Arkansas river, the State will choose. As Jon stays in the house, trying to hold back, his tear, while cleaning up orange plasma, from Terra's corpse and Benjamin's bleeding still. But Jon is, already misses his dad, as well as his mother, the house, that him and Sheila grew up in is, now, a tomb of memories, that had, a twist of fate, from evil ones, that holds so much of wickedness for a family, that meant, for good and wonderful things, but Terra and her father, kept, the war going, by dragging innocent people into, the situation, to harm them. For Ed and Sam could have, talk all this over, a cup of coffee, to resolved this hatred, towards, each other, But when Ed, decided, to kidnap Sheila, and holds her hostage, that anger Sam. So Sam holds, Terra in the meantime, for his hostage. Well two evils don't make a good, neither right. See Terra, ideal had back fired on her, when she thought of, getting everyone in one spot, to execute, them all. But Dana, was right again, Terra's plots never work, when her and her protégé, wasn't on the same page. Terra say go right, then she goes left, so she contradicts herself every time. And that's her downfall, not just her down fall, but the death of her.

So again, the good in people, always prevailed against, the bad, the evil and the ugly wickedness, and it doesn't require much, to do good, because, good speaks, a different language then it's counterpart (evil). But matter how much evil, outweigh, the good, but just a tittle of good, will go a long way. But also, the heaviness of good can conquer, all territories and depresses evil into, the ground, because, evil's powers are limited and it's needs, are weaker individuals, to hoist on, that needs help in overcoming, the wickedness by feeding on a good conversation, for purification. Sometimes it takes, a soft-spoken words, that can turn away negative, hostility, evil and malicious ways. There is, those old saying "Game recognized Game" that evil loves misery, with its own, at the top. But greatness, will stand alone, tall and strong, with a humble spirit. Because, greatness almost inherited, the kingdom of God: But Christ said, the difference is, the Lord God, and there it is. There isn't nothing greater, then God, he is superior to all of Heaven and everything here on, this planet, that is called earth.

No Legacy To Spare
Chapter XII

Spring weather has come into Lajunta, like never before, with the sun shining and, the air is just right, for picnic or a delicious cookout. It seems, that everybody, was enjoying, the weather, that God has given them. With smiles, all over, the place So it was, a unique day, to give thanks, for being alive, and having great people, to respond too. It was, a unique day for Ms. Dana Lynn, to go, to trial, for her crimes, she had committed. As the courtroom, being fill, to capacity. The Bentford's are witness in this glorious day, for the prosecutors is to make sure, that she gets, the death penalty, against her. And all the evident, are sticking, to her like glue, to wood, and the prosecution team isn't letting up one bit by throwing the state book, at her. The Judge isn't taking, this case lightly at all. As hearing, from both sides, Dana's lawyer didn't have a chance, to plea her case. It seems, that he knew, that she was guilty as well. But today, justices, was working like it suppose too, on criminal's and for the community. Not the other way around. Sometimes there are flaws, with the manmade system, with justices works against hard working people, then to being for them, like convicting, a mother, for feeding her kids then to letting, a criminal out of jail, to kill his baby's mother. So the Justices system is lawful, and no good at all. It only works, for certain people, and that's a load of crap, to hear and to say. In today's society, you better not, at all speak on, the truth, because, they that do it, is known, as outcast, and expected, to be remove, from the face of the earth. As the previous generations of people, that was here, to do a job, and was assassinated, got very sick and couldn't recover or dismember someone's body, to no trace, and can't be found.

Now Cain, was asked, to testify, against, his former and decease boss, about the killings, that were committed by Terra and her accomplice Ms. Dana Lynn. Their first victim, was that he brought, to the jury was Mr. Robert (Bobby) Raoul, which both women killed him, for taking photos of another woman, that Terra didn't care for. "Terra hated, Sheila, and the feeling we're mutual, between her and Sheila." said, Cain Gordillo. "Then they always, had talk about getting Mr. Samuel Bentford, so she could kill him, because, her father was killed, by them, so as she always said, a father, for a father." said, Cain. As the prosecution team, hitting all cylinders, from top to bottom and side to side, this case isn't going quite right, for Dana Lynn, but this case, will be over in a mount of hours, the way everything is going isn't good, for Dana. As they put Mr. Benjamin Tills on the stand, Dana was very surprised, to hear, what he had, to say. As he stresses, "a point, that Cain had givin early, that both women had contemplating on killing my brother-in-law, as they held us both hostages." said, Benjamin. "I was shot twice, by Terra in my foot and once in my arm, they had kidnap me, because, they thought, that I was Sam, at one point, that day, I thought, that I was going, to die, but I had them both believing, that I was Sam's Insurance salesmen, and I told, them both that Sam was selling, his truck to me, they didn't know, that I was, a former detective in, the state of Hawaii, I didn't want, to blow my cover, at all, because, if I would had, told, them, that I was, a former cop, they would probably kill me." said, Benjamin. "But they wanted my brother-in-law, so that, they could kill him sooner, the better." said, Benjamin. The Prosecution team, they still have, the floor and Dana's lawyer hasn't object, to anything, because, the Prosecution team, has already, has the jury attention on all that is being said.

So that every charge will stick, and for every count her sentencing probably double. Now for every murder, she committed, the Judge will give her ten years. Like she murdered a father and five sons, her fiancée and his harlot, Bobby Raoul, and she accompany Terra in the killing of Mr. Nual Reyes henchmen's, and Mr. Samuel Bentford, in who is, a well-known individual in town. As the Judge looks on her, with no pity at all, but Dana shows no remorse at all, for what she has done. The Jury, see a troubled individual, that needs, to get what she did to other, that is, to be put to sleep. Why waste a dime of, the tax payer's money, by putting her in a cell, for free meals and showers. Now her lawyer, wants a venue for a new trial, to have it in another part of Colorado. There will not be a hung jury. Every one of the twelve jury members that knows, Sam and his family, are on board, to see that she gets, the proper sentencing, and that is lethal injection. It's too bad, that Terra isn't here, for her trial, which her sentencing would have been very devastating. Now the jury has reach, it's verdict. All members have found Dana Lynn "GUILTY!" on all counts, the courtroom was in a clapping venge, and a happy crowd, to the decision, that was made. The Judge was all smiles, to that as well, until he forgot, to use his gavel, to quieted, the courtroom. But when, a retired cop hit the stand, that's when the law is very heavy on, the defendant, for shooting a retired cop, the law will take care of its own. By Benjamin, being who he is, her sentences, got much more heavier, then usual. The Judge, and his courtroom didn't wait, so why wait, for tomorrow, for what you can do today, and this Judge, the courtroom, the prosecution team and Jury, were, a team, that God himself, had put in place, to take care of an evil and wicked somebody, that is so diabolical, that needs, to be removed, from society, way of life.

Since Terra, being dead, the Judge was making sure, that, the courts, will handle Terra's death situation, to see that her remains, are cremated, since there isn't, any form of immediate family. Terra was, the only child, that Ed and Terri produce. "So before, I give, your sentences are, there anything you like, to say to this court?" ask, the Judge. "Yes,

I like, to ask you, who in the f**k! are you to judge me, you son of b**ches!! nobody knows, what I been through!!" said, Dana. As the Judge, handing down her sentencing, as she stood, there crying, with mad emotions, all she can do is, be mad at herself, going out, to doing all, the wrong and devious things, to indulge, themselves, to make them absolutely invincible, then when the smoke clears, the same people or individuals wants you, to have some compassion, for them as well. How can, that be!? But to, a few it's ok, But the rest of society, has to give in, and help clean up, the mess, the inconsiderate ones that made it happened. Though no one made them, to do it.

Now that, the newspaper reporters and news anchors, are getting everything in perspective, about, the trial, and the missing piece of the puzzle, was Terra's story on how she, became, a diabolical being, and what had driven her, to be that way. But being, the daughter of Edward Dart a retired engineer, for, a train company many years ago, until he bought himself his owned automotive car parts store. Then he was also murdered, by the same family in, which was defending themselves against him. But the newspapers wrote, the word "Deja vu" in retrospect, of father and daughters acts of violence, are so similar, to one another, and their death's as well.

So once again, that good had conquered, and overcome evil again, with many times over. With love, respect, meekness and of course humility. With all that wrapped up into one, can make, a powerful weapon against evil. Proverbs had told, you once, that anxiety weighs down the heart, but a kind word cheers it up. Now that two years is, approaching, Jon has made up his mind into moving on, and leaving, all the miserable memories behind him, to moving, to Arizona, for a sound peace of mind, and starting all over, for a new life. Jon spoke briefly on missing his parents and having fond memories of growing up in the house, that his, father and mother had made for him and Sheila. But Jon, had thought of staying in Colorado, but the memories, he couldn't bear. While Cain and Sheila, had talk, about moving also, but further east. But the one thing, that is for sure is, being married, before, they could move on. And Sheila, even told, Cain that she would like, a couple of children, with him, but must be married first. And Cain had promised, to do great into, taking care of Sheila and his babies. Now for Benjamin, he was planning on sticking around and looking, for some part time work, with the Lajunta Sheriff's office. And find him, a one-bedroom condo, and settle down, with a new female companion. With his foot and arm being wounded, he had to go to, a rehabilitation, to be able, to walk again and to use his arm as well. The following year later, that Nual, was killed, by his arch rivalry, to take over his territory. This was, a sanction decision, for to hit a man, like Nual, it came from, the top of his organization. Nual wasn't making, the money like he uses too, so they had him rubout. Everyone, that was around him, had to keep their mouths shut, and not say a word, and let things be. Nual, wasn't running his family like his superiors, wanted him to run it. So they said, that Nual's time was up, with the organization. Running, his family reckless, and skimming his bosses cut of the money, from his racket's profits, and lying about it. So they sent people, to watch him and his family, and Nual wasn't aware, that he was being watched, all the time. And Nual also had, a brush in with I.R.S, for back taxes on his millions he made, from his gambling and auto theft rackets. So the organization knows, that he was holding out on them as well. The commission, tried, to reason, with Nual into paying what he owed them.

But their talking gotten no where, because, Nual had told, his bosses, to go and screw, themselves, and each other, while at it. So Nual's demised, was brought upon himself. And Nual will be replace by, a person, that is a little transparent, then Mr. Reyes was. See the one thing, that Nual had really forgotten, that is, the syndicate owns him, and not the other way around. But definitely the commission, had to make, an example out of one of their own, for others, that is within, the organization, to take heed, and live by the sword, then die by the sword. While Migual knows, that his cousin had being killed, Migual had, to let things be, for him to stay alive, and keep his diner opened, to the community. But one slip up, and he could end up, like his cousin. Migual was warn, about talking, too much, about the commission business, with other people, that he shouldn't trust. As the powers to be, was coming to shake up things, that Nual was suppose, to do.

But didn't do, Because, he was too busy, showboating his luxury lifestyle. As under Nual's leadership, many men have died unexpected to his missed information, that he had. And not question his motives, or send his under boss, to look into it. He would, send his henchmen, to kill. So he would solve, a problem, with a barrel of, the gun, then with talking things over. That wasn't, the way, to run, an outfit, for the commission, to have innocent blood, to be shaded, and lives could have been spared.

So with that said, Terra McKenzie is gone, and joining her parents in death. Terra could've been, a sweet person, but refuses, to change her evil and wicked ways. With her father's evil side growing in her, wasn't meant for her, to be good and meek. The more Terra holds, the evil, the more wickedness she becomes. So therefore, no legacy, for her to spare, even though, she was Ed's child, to keep his legacy going but evil does has, a limited time, to reign on earth, as always. Nual was sort of, a good guy, but also ruthless at times on his short comings, but doesn't mind helping others, that are in needed of a hand. But if he would've lived, just a little longer the community knows Nual could have make a difference, but also for him no legacy, to spare, because, his evil doings have caught up, with him, for the people, to know what he was all about. The lifestyle, that these individuals live, wasn't indeed pretty at all. But the bad memories, that they left behind for it, to dwell in the heads of people, that thought good about them. But also the people, that has cross, their paths is the ones, that has a nightmare, that death was knocking at the door, and didn't know, when to answer it. But Samuel Bentford has every bit of, a legacy, to spare, with Jon and Sheila as very good people, to make that happened. With Sam's two seeds, he had a bunch of grandchildren. Because, Jon and his wife, had three children, and they had a bunch of children. Sheila and Cain, had two sons' and they also had a bunch of children. So Sam's seeds, grew into a huge generation of Bentford's everywhere, with a tight knitted family, that nothing can conquer love and good, when a family is for good. Ms. Dana Lynn on the other hand, was put to death, by lethal injection, for all her crime activity she, allowed herself, to do. But no legacy, definitely, for her. So for, all the wanna be bad people, that has life, all figured out, by doing so much wrong, and getting away, with it. The judgment is coming, and you don't know when. There was, a man name Paul, that told, me, that after sin is finished, there is death waiting for you, at the door.

So God, has blessed, this family, to where, they were very fruitful and they have multiple into a fun-loving family. With Sam and June, side by side looking down on their seeds, from love, hope, peace and prosperity.

The heart is deceitful above all things, and desperately wicked: Who can know it? Jeremiah 17:9.

The End